FOLK ARTS
Around the World

FOLK ARTS
Around the World
And How to Make Them

VIRGINIE FOWLER

illustrations by the author

Prentice-Hall, Inc. / *Englewood Cliffs, New Jersey*

Prentice-Hall International, Inc., London
Prentice-Hall of Australia, Pty. Ltd., North Sydney
Prentice-Hall of Canada, Ltd., Toronto
Prentice-Hall of India Private Ltd., New Delhi
Prentice-Hall of Japan, Inc., Tokyo
Prentice-Hall of Southeast Asia Pte. Ltd., Singapore
Whitehall Books Limited, Wellington, New Zealand
10 9 8 7 6 5 4 3 2 1

Library of Congress Cataloging in Publication Data
Fowler, Virginie.
Folk arts around the world.
   Includes index.
Summary: Describes traditional folk crafts
of countries around the world with instructions
for making several crafts from each country.
   1. Handicraft—Juvenile literature.
[1. Handicraft. 2. Folk art] I. Title.
TT160.E43 745.5 80-26681 ISBN 0-13-323014-7

To David Jeffrey Rothwell
his book

Contents

Folk Arts: What Are They?

Folk arts are the things people have made with their hands from available raw materials. Originally these were objects needed in daily life. Families living in remote farm areas built their own houses and made their furniture; tools were made from wood and metal; pots and dishes were formed of clay and wood. People wove and dyed their own fabrics for clothes and blankets and created toys for children's play. These designs were handed down from generation to generation. In some places of the world this is still a way of life; and many people are re-learning these skills as a satisfying way of creating needed objects rather than buying factory ones.

Gradually, as people came together in villages and towns, skilled craftspeople specialized in one craft—woodworking, pottery, weaving, metalwork, printing of fabrics, glass blowing, papermaking, and many variations of these basic crafts. This led to new designs, and sometimes to more elaborate decorations.

The line between folk art and fine art narrowed, as objects were made for their beauty alone, not just for use, but for pure adornment of person or house or church. Fine jewelers, working with gold and precious metals, and weavers of elaborately designed silk tapestries brought the skills of the craftsperson to a high level of art. At the same time they had not lost touch with the basic craft of working with their hands to create an object from a raw material.

Designs and decorations of folk arts change from country to country, depending on what raw materials are available, and what objects fit into the needs of the people. The decorations also are derived from the life that is seen by the craftsperson. The animals and plants that are part of the countryside, the seashells of the coastal countries, the ways of farming and travel, the look of the landscape—all these go into the designs that are handed down from generation to generation.

A country's climate and living conditions play a part in craft designs and objects. The weavers in hot countries make thin fabrics that are comfortable to wear. Silk and cotton are raw products of these countries and are made into lightweight fabrics. The dyes come from roots, barks, and plants that grow nearby; the designs reflect the vivid colors of the flowers and the bold shapes of leaves.

In cold countries the cloth is a heavy woolen, woven from warm sheep's wool, waterproofed against cold, soaking rains with the sheep's own hair oil called lanolin. The colors are often the dull colors of the natural wool, or local bark dyes which are tans and grays.

Where wood is plentiful, objects are made from wood. In these countries clay is also fired (baked) at a high temperature in large wood-burning ovens called kilns; the final result is stoneware and porcelain. Centuries ago, Chinese hillsides were stripped of wood to make high-fired clay objects. Where there are few forests, clay objects have to be low-fired, and are usually made of a red clay which hardens under low heat.

Some of the designs in this book are very old, and the original pieces are in museums. Other folk art designs are still made in their countries, and some designs have developed through years of working with a material. But all the designs are authentically part of the folk art crafts of each country. A short paragraph or two describes the origin of each design and how it came to be part of a country's heritage.

Some projects are easy to make; others are a little harder to do. In the Table of Contents, look for the projects marked "easy." And since these are folk art crafts, the tools and materials used are very simple. Often the tools are kitchen ones, or standard household items. For some of the designs, modern shortcuts are used, especially for dyes, clays, metalwork, and woodwork.

In using kitchen tools, check with an older person to see if you may use them. *And* also check with an older person if you plan to use the stove, electric iron, or cutting knives. As a good craftsperson always does, wear an apron when working, and cover the working surface with newspapers.

Before You Begin

❖❖❖

At the beginning of each section you will find instructions on the handling of the basic materials for the projects.

There are two processes that are used in all the sections; they are described here in the beginning of the book. Whenever you need to enlarge or transfer a design, refer to the following instructions on Enlarging and Transferring. Many projects are painted, and you will find instructions in the section on Painting. Turn to this section whenever you have to paint, shellac, or varnish a design.

Enlarging and Transferring Designs

Enlarging

The patterns for each project are drawn to scale on a grid. The enlarging information is printed just below the lower right-hand corner of the pattern. Increase the size of the squares of the grid to the measurement shown—½ inch, ¾ inch, or 1 inch.

On typewriter paper or *graph paper*, measure and draw larger squares, matching the enlarging information; number the lines. If the enlarged drawing is larger than a sheet of typewriter paper, hold several sheets together with tape to make one large sheet. You can also use ¼-inch squared graph paper. Count off the number of squares needed for the enlargement, and with a ruler and pencil draw the vertical and horizontal lines. For instance, for an enlargement to 1-inch squares, count off four ¼-inch squares and make a heavy pencil line. Number the lines.

5

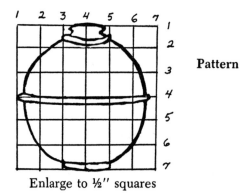

Pattern

Enlarge to ½″ squares

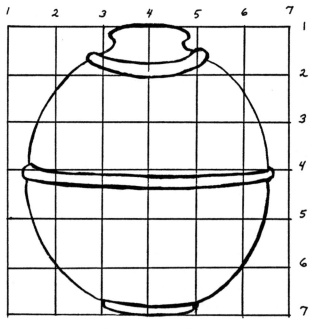

Enlarged Drawing

Now all you have to do is draw in the lines of the pattern drawing on the larger squares, following the lines on the smaller grid. Draw across each square in the same place, and cut across each grid line at the same place. When you are finished, you will have an exact enlargement of the original pattern.

To reduce a drawing, make the final grid on the typewriter paper smaller than the original pattern grid.

Transferring a drawing

After you have made the enlarged pattern by the grid method, transfer it to the final material of the project. In most cases you will use *graphite paper*, which is better than *carbon paper*. The transferring side of graphite paper has the same surface as lead pencil, so any lines can be erased. Carbon paper has a waxy surface which cannot be erased easily without smudging.

Place graphite paper, black side down, on the material of the project. Hold in place with four small pieces of masking tape. Put the pattern design on top of the graphite paper. Hold it in place with pieces of masking tape.

Now, with a sharp-pointed #3 (hard) lead pencil, trace over all the lines of the pattern, except the grid lines. You can also use a ballpoint pen. Before removing the pattern and graphite paper, loosen one or two pieces of masking tape and peek under the graphite paper. Check carefully to see if all lines have been transferred. If not, go over the ones you have missed. If all lines are in place, remove the pattern drawing and graphite paper. Proceed with the project.

Painting

Acrylic paint

The best all-around paint for the projects in this book is acrylic paint. It can be thinned with water or acrylic polymer medium for a transparent look; it can be applied thickly so as to be opaque; it is waterproof, so it can be used on washable fabrics; and it dries quickly.

Buy acrylic paint in tubes. Use the color directly from the tube, or mix two colors together to form another color. For instance, if you have one tube of blue and one of yellow, mix equal amounts together to make green.

Before starting to mix paint, cover the working surface with several sheets of newspaper. Have extra papers handy so you can cover any spilled paint with fresh paper.

Mix water with the paint to form a transparent color. The more water you add, the thinner and lighter the color will be. Always have an extra sheet beside you of the same paper, cloth, or other material as the final project on which to test the paint. Since acrylic paint dries very quickly, use throwaway containers for mixing pans— individual aluminum foil cupcake pans are good, or small plastic drinking cups. After putting on the first coat of paint, let it dry before adding the second coat. To keep a special mixed color from drying out, put the paint in a small jar with a tight fitting cover. This way, the paint will be liquid for the second coat.

There are two acrylic *polymer mediums* that can be used with acrylic paints. One is *gloss* which is added to the paint as a thinner; it gives the paint a high gloss when dry. The other is *matte,* which lessens the shine of the paint. Both can be used as a final varnish coat over the paint. The gloss can also be used as a glue for paper or decoupage work.

When stenciling paper or other materials, use the acrylic paint right from the tube without thinning. Squeeze the color out on a flat plastic cover from a coffee can, or similar type of flat plastic cover.

Always wipe off the screw top and the cap of a paint tube right after using. Otherwise the cap will stick and will be hard to take off the tube the next time you use the paint. Do the same for the jars of gloss or matte medium.

In the projects using acrylic paint, you will need soft nylon brushes, either flat or round, as they do not leave brush marks on the paint. The exception is a stencil brush, which is round with a flat bottom and is made of stiff bristles. Always keep a jar of clean water beside you when you work. Keep the brushes in the water when you are not using them so any paint will not harden on the bristles. Wipe off the water with a cloth or face tissue before dipping the brush in the color. When you are through, wash the brush thoroughly with soap and water. If the paint does dry on a brush, use denatured alcohol to remove it.

Enamel paint

Enamel paint is sold in paint and hardware stores, variety stores, craft and art stores. Craft stores sell small 2-ounce jars of hobby enamel. Household type enamel is sold in cans, with the smallest being 8 ounces. Read the manufacturer's directions and warnings on the can.

Open the can or jar of enamel and stir it with a small wooden stick. Keep stirring until the enamel has reached an even color, and there are no streaks of oil showing in the mixture.

Dip a soft watercolor brush into the enamel, halfway up the brush area. Scrape the brush lightly against the top inside edge of the can or jar to take off extra liquid. Draw the brush in an even stroke over the surface to be painted, letting the enamel flow easily. Do not brush over the enamel with back-and-forth motions. Cover all the surface with the enamel. Let the enamel dry until it is hard. Then add a second coat if needed. Drying time usually depends on the weather, so there is no hard and fast time of drying.

While the first coat is drying, wash the brush (and your hands) with turpentine until clean. Tightly cover the jar or can of enamel so no air can get in. It is a good idea to pour just a little turpentine on top of the enamel before putting on the cover. This will prevent a skin forming on the surface. If a skin has formed on the top of the enamel, lift it up, all in one piece, with a wooden stirrer, and throw it away.

White shellac

White shellac is a thin, almost colorless liquid. It is used on wood as a first coat to seal the surface. Sometimes this is the only finish used on wood. As a sealer, it forms a base coat for the final paint or enamel finish. Shellac is used also as a final coat over wood stain, paint on paper, or decoupage on paper, to form a protective finish.

Shellac does not have to be stirred. Flow it on evenly with a soft watercolor brush without brushing back over the surface. It will dry very quickly. When it is dry, sandpaper the surface with medium sandpaper. Put on another coat, let dry, and sandpaper again, if this is a base coat. If this is the finish, do not sandpaper the surface.

Immediately after using shellac, clean off the brush with denatured alcohol.

Polyurethane varnish

This is an absolutely colorless varnish sold in 8-ounce and larger cans at paint and hardware stores. It can be used as a substitute for shellac; apply it in the same way with a soft, flat watercolor brush (see White shellac above). Follow the manufacturer's directions on the can, and note any warnings.

Where to Buy Supplies
Many of the supplies needed for the projects are found in your home, in the kitchen, desk, sewing cabinet, or family workshop. Check around the house, and ask permission to use tools or supplies before buying anything new.

Craft supplies listed in this book can be bought from an art store, hobby shop, or model-making shop. These supplies include clay, acrylic paints and acrylic polymer mediums, paper, brushes, ink, balsa wood, stencil and graphite paper, and all sorts of other supplies, including art and craft tools.

Hardware or paint stores are good places to buy shellac, enamel paints, and polyurethane varnish. Some stores carry wood dowels and small strips of balsa or other lightweight wood. Many of these supplies are sold at the lumberyard or wood shop.

Fabrics are found in fabric shops or department stores, where you can also buy beads, sequins, and buttons. Many variety stores and trimming shops also carry these supplies.

You will find that most supplies are sold only in standard quantities. However, these supplies are used in several projects. For instance, oven-baked clay is sold in either 2- or 3½-pound boxes depending on the manufacturer, but a box of clay is enough to make all the clay projects in this book. Tools, too, are used for many different projects.

If you do not know where the local stores are, look in the Yellow Pages of the telephone directory under Craft Supplies; Hobby and Model Construction Supplies; Artist's Materials and Supplies; Fabric Shops; Notions—Retail; Lumber—Retail; Paint—Retail; Hardware.

All craft people have to buy some of their supplies by mail order, as local stores often do not carry the exact product that is needed for a project. Send for the catalogs of the suppliers listed in the back of the book. Then choose those supplies you will need, and send for them.

Clay Folk Arts

✤ ✤ ✤

Techniques of Working with Clay
The clay crafts described in this book are all made from a special type
of clay, called *oven-baked*. It is sold in 2- to 3½-pound boxes, and is
made by several manufacturers. It looks, feels, and can be formed
just like regular clay. It is baked in the kitchen oven at 250° F for less
than two hours. The colored or clear *glaze* finish is brushed on, then
air-dried. Acrylic paint can also be used as a finish coat.

The clay objects will not be as strong as those baked at high
temperatures in a regular clay oven called a *kiln*. However, the
objects described in this book are all decorative and are not meant
for daily use.

The craft of working with clay is called *potting*; the objects made
are called *pots*, no matter what their shape or use; the craftsperson is
called a *potter*.

Clay-working tools
All the clay projects in this book, except one, are made from slabs
of clay. You will need only a few tools—most of them found in the
kitchen.

You will need:
a plastic cleaner's bag—24 x 30 inches
two pieces of wood lathe—15 x 2 x ½ inches
two pieces of wood lathe—15 x 2 x ¼ inches
a small plastic (or wood) rolling pin

a small bowl for water
a piece of cellulose sponge—3 x 3 x ¾ inches
a kitchen paring knife
a small spoon
assorted dishes as molds
a metal cookie sheet
a separate oven thermometer
flat watercolor brush—¾ inch wide
small plastic bowls to mix glazes in
typewriter paper for patterns
pencil, ruler, and scissors
oven mitts or padded pot holders
medium sandpaper

Rolling out clay

When you begin a project, take out a little more clay than you will need for the pot. It is better to work with too much clay than too little. The unused clay can be put back into a plastic bag, a twistem tied around the opening, and then put back into the box to be used for another project. A 2- or 3½-pound box will make several of the projects in this book.

Form the clay into a ball; then flatten the ball with the palms of your hands. Place the flattened piece of clay in the center of a moistened plastic cleaner's bag, which is spread out on the working surface. Lay two pieces of lathe flat on each side of the clay 7 to 12 inches apart, depending on the project, and parallel to each other, going away from you. Have a bowl of water and the sponge beside you on the plastic. These are to moisten the clay and the rolling pin as needed. If the clay and the rolling pin get too dry, they will stick together. But do not use too much water, or you'll have a mud pie.

Roll the clay, from the center outward, with a slow, even pressure. Each stroke is at a different angle, as if you are following the hands of a clock all around the circle. If the edges crack, moisten the crack lightly with the sponge dipped in water; press the edges together with your fingers and continue rolling. Try to keep the shape as near to a square or rectangle as possible. When the ends of the rolling pin finally run on the top of the wooden lathes, you are done. Your slab of clay is now an even thickness throughout—½ inch or ¼ inch, the same thickness as the lathes you are using.

Remove the lathes, and mop up any excess water on the plastic with the sponge.

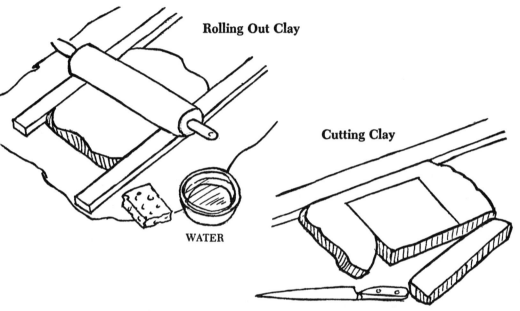

Rolling Out Clay

Cutting Clay

WATER

Cutting and molding clay

Lay the paper pattern over the clay and cut around the edges with a sharp-pointed paring knife. Lift up the pattern and remove any extra clay around the edges. Use this extra clay for any pieces that are to be added to the project; otherwise return extra clay to the box and seal the box so the clay will not dry out. Let all the patterned pieces of clay dry for four to seven hours before removing them from the plastic sheet.

Always make all parts of a clay project at once, so each part dries at the same time. This is important if one part is to be stuck to another part, as they have to be equally dry. A moist piece of clay will not *permanently* become part of a semi-dry piece. It will drop off when baked.

When the clay is firm, but still soft, remove it from the plastic sheet. (The length of time needed for drying is not always the same; it depends on whether the air in the room is dry or moist, hot or cold.) If the clay is too stiff, it cannot be formed over the *mold*. Lift the clay carefully, gently pulling the plastic away from the bottom as you lift.

Drape the slab of clay over whatever mold you are using for the project. With the paring knife, cut away the extra clay that hangs over the bottom edge of the mold. Let the clay dry until it holds its shape; then remove it from the mold. If the clay gets too dry, it will be hard to remove from the mold, since clay shrinks as it dries.

Attaching clay pieces

At this point, add any extra pieces to the main part of the pot, using *slip* to attach them.

Slip is made by mixing water and clay in a small bowl, until it is as thick as molasses. This mixture is dabbed and smoothed on the clay surface where a piece is to be added. Also put slip on the joining surface of the piece or pieces to be added. Press the two pieces together, and let dry a bit; then smooth the joint with slip until any joining cracks disappear.

Making a foot

If you are making a *tile*, lift it away from the plastic sheet, as you did the slab for a mold. Turn the tile over and cut a *foot*, which is a narrow bottom edge for a tile or pot. With the pencil and ruler, draw a line ½ inch in from the edge and ⅛ inch deep around all four sides. Using a small spoon, scoop out the clay inside this edge, to the ⅛-inch depth. This will leave a ½-inch wide foot all around the edge of the tile. The shallow air space created by the foot will keep the tile from warping or cracking during baking.

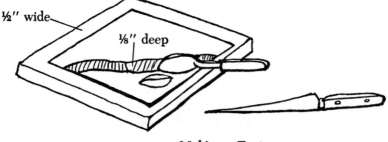

½″ wide

⅛″ deep

Making a Foot

Follow the same procedure in making a foot for a pot; however, make the width of the bottom edge ⅛ to ¼ inch.

Drying clay

Let your clay pot or tile dry until it is stiff. The clay should still be slightly moist, not powdery and hard; this stage is called *leather-hard.* Go over the surface with a dampened sponge to smooth out any cracks or rough places. This is also the time to cut a foot in the bottom of a pot, *if* you have not added a foot of extra clay to a thin-bottomed pot. (See previous paragraph for directions.)

When the clay object is totally dry, in two or three days, smooth the surface with sandpaper. Work carefully, as the object will be very brittle at this stage.

Baking clay

Put the clay object on a clean baking pan or cookie sheet. Place a baking thermometer beside it, so you can watch the temperature. Put the pan, object, and thermometer in the middle of the kitchen oven. Turn on the heat to low, but leave the door open. Let the pot dry at 150° F for 30 minutes. Then almost close the oven door, leaving a 2-inch crack. Turn up the heat to 250°. Open the door every so often and check the heat, so that it does not go above or below 250°. The pot should stay in the oven for 30 to 45 minutes, depending on the manufacturer's directions. Turn off the heat, open the door, and let the pot cool down in the oven.

If you do not follow this slow drying and baking process, the clay object may crack or shatter into small pieces. Any extra moisture left in the clay will expand into steam and break through the dry outside surface.

Painting or glazing clay

When the pot is cool, take it out of the oven. Cover the surface with clear glaze or colored glaze, following the manufacturer's directions. Each type of clay has its own glaze formula. Glazes are sold in ¾-ounce bottles, and the colors can be mixed together or mixed with clear glaze. A flat ¾-inch wide watercolor brush is best for applying the glazes.

You may need several coats of glaze, as thin coats are best. Let each coat dry in the air before adding the next one. Even though the manufacturer suggests drying the glazes in the oven, air-drying works better.

You can also decorate the pot with acrylic paints.

Extra tip

If you have to leave a clay project for a few days before it is finished, wrap it in a piece of plastic cleaning bag. This will keep the moisture in the clay so it will not dry out too much.

CAMEROON GRAIN CONTAINER

The original of this jar is huge—eight feet or so high, higher than a man. These jars are used to store grain in the villages of northern Cameroon in West Africa. They are made of two bowl-like sections.

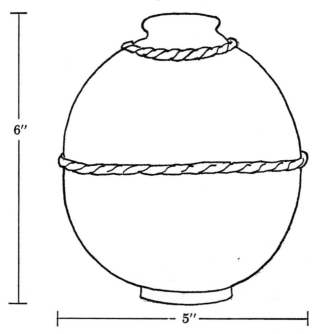

Ropes of clay are coiled round and round until each section is finished. The surface of the clay is smoothed, inside and out. Then the sections are put together, one being up-ended over the other. A rope of clay is put over the joint.

For this miniature container, the clay will be rolled out into a slab and formed over two matching bowl molds.

Materials and Tools
3½-pound box of oven-baked clay
2 small bowls—5 inches in diameter, 2½ inches high
2 jars—4 to 6 inches high
clay-working tools
compass
transparent glaze (optional)

Directions
1. Roll the clay to a ¼-inch thick slab, 10 x 20 inches, using ¼-inch lathes.
2. Cut the slab in half with a knife. Let the two halves dry until they can be handled.
3. Turn the bowls upside down, and put each one over the top of a jar. Place each slab of clay over an upturned bowl. Trim away extra clay around the edges of the bowls. Press clay close to the bowls so the surface is smooth and even.

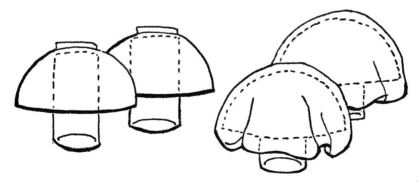

Step 3

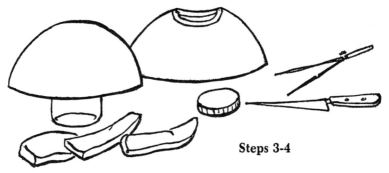

Steps 3-4

4. When the clay is partially dry and will hold its shape, remove from the bowls. First, remove one clay shape from its bowl, and place it upright on the working surface for further drying. Then draw a small circle, 1¾ inches in diameter, with the compass on the center bottom of the second clay bowl shape. Cut out the circle with a sharp-pointed knife. Put this circle of clay to one side. Now remove the second clay bowl from its mold. Turn upright to dry a bit.

5. Trim the circle of clay, removed from the bottom of the second bowl, so that it fits the outside bottom of the first clay bowl. Attach the circle with clay slip. Cut away some of the interior of the clay circle to the depth of ⅛ inch. Leave a ⅜-inch wide rim around the edge. This is the foot of the bowl.

6. The next step is to attach the two bowls to one another. Smear clay slip around the edges of each bowl. Lightly but firmly, press the edges of the bowls against each other. With a finger dipped in water, smooth the joint until the crack is closed.

Step 5   SLIP   **Step 6**

7. Roll a long, thin coil of clay, about ¼ inch in diameter, with the palms of your hands. It should be long enough to go around the joint area (about 17 inches long). Attach the roll of clay to the joint with clay slip. Roll a second, shorter coil of clay. This will be attached to the top of the jar in the next step.

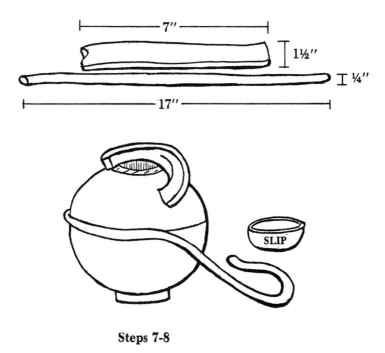

Steps 7-8

8. With a knife, cut a 1½-inch wide strip of clay, 7 inches long. Attach this strip, with slip, around the open hole at the top of the jar. Curve the strip inward, then up and out in a flared edge—see drawing. Remove any excess clay at the seam. Use slip to attach the second coil of clay to the joint between jar and strip of clay.

9. Let the jar dry thoroughly. Smooth out any rough spots with a damp sponge when the clay is leather-hard. When the jar is completely dry, bake it in the oven.

10. Grain jars do not have any glaze on the surface, so the jar is done when it has been baked. If you want to cover the surface, use a transparent glaze and let it dry in the air.

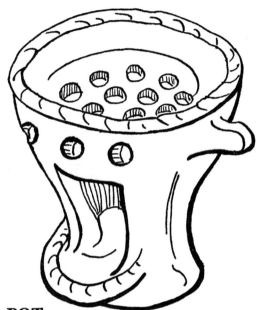

CARIBBEAN COAL-POT

On St. Lucia, a Caribbean island south of Martinique, food is cooked over a clay coal-pot. This is a type of charcoal cooker used by the Carib Indians long before the Europeans settled the island. It is made of a very low-fired red clay. Coal-pots are 12 to 14 inches high, with the top charcoal-containing basin about that width. A metal grill to hold a pot is often put over the charcoal area; or meat pushed onto sticks is held over the fire; or a whole breadfruit is roasted on top of the coals. Ashes drop down through the holes in the basin and are scraped out through an opening in the base. The coal-pot in this project is a miniature one—about 4 inches high, with a charcoal basin about 4½ inches across and 1 inch deep.

Materials and Tools
2-pound box of terra-cotta color oven-baked clay
1 sheet of typewriter paper
glass or plastic bowl—4½ inches in diameter
small frozen orange juice can
clay-working tools
compass

Directions

1. With the compass, draw three circles on the typewriter paper—diameters are 6 inches, 5 inches, and 2¼ inches. Cut out the circles with scissors.

2. Roll out a ¼-inch thick slab of clay, 7½ x 17 inches, using two ¼-inch lathes.

3. Place the paper circles over the clay slab and cut around the edges with a sharp-pointed knife. Also cut a rectangle, 2½ x 7½ inches. Let the clay pieces dry until they can be handled.

4. Dip the bottom of the bowl in water, turn it over, and drape the 6-inch circle of clay over the bottom and down the sides. Trim edge until the side area is 2 inches deep, and even with the bottom edge of the bowl. Cut out a 2¼-inch center circle from the top. Set circle of clay aside.

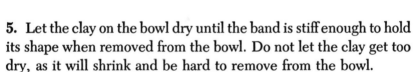

Step 4

5. Let the clay on the bowl dry until the band is stiff enough to hold its shape when removed from the bowl. Do not let the clay get too dry, as it will shrink and be hard to remove from the bowl.

6. Meanwhile, wrap the rectangle of clay around the orange juice can. Seal the edges with slip. Let dry until it can be removed from the can.

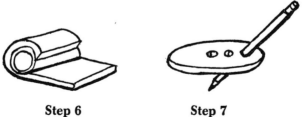

Step 6   Step 7

7. Gently curve the 5-inch circle into a shallow bowl shape, about 1 inch deep in the center. With a pencil, punch twelve or thirteen holes in the bottom of the bowl.

8. Remove the clay tube from the orange juice can. Remove the circular band from the bowl. Attach the shallow bowl to the clay band with slip. Attach the smaller end of the band to one open end of the tube. Smooth the joint with clay slip, curving the band into the tube.

Step 8

Step 9

Step 10

9. Cut a 1½-inch square in the front of the tube. Angle the sides inward as you make the cut with a knife.

10. Fold the 2¼-inch circle (from Step 4) in half. Form a scooped-out lip of clay with a curled-up edge in front of and a little below the square opening in the tube. The bottom of the lip should not be as low as the bottom of the tube. Attach this lip to the tube with slip (see drawing).

11. Attach the 2¼-inch circle of clay (from Step 1) to the bottom of the tube. Use slip to attach the circle, and curve the circle upward so that the center is about ⅜ inch above the bottom edge of the tube. Add a small piece of rolled-out clay to the bottom of the cut-out area, just above the lip, and inside the tube. This is where the charcoal ashes drop down and are scraped out into the lip. Punch a small hole in the center of the bottom covering of the tube, so that any hot air

Steps 11-13

that might collect at the bottom of the tube between the two layers of clay will not explode the clay. Nick the edge of the bowl at the top with a knife.

12. Roll out two strips of clay, 2½ inches long and ¾ inch wide. Fold the strips in half crosswise. Press and smooth the ends into the opposite sides of the pot, ½ inch down from the top rim. Pinch the outer ends to a rounded point (see drawing).

13. Finally, use a pencil to punch three holes across the front, just above the square opening. The holes should go right through to the center shallow bowl. The center of the holes should be about ¾ inch above the square opening (see drawing). The three holes and the bottom opening seem to make a face, with the side pieces as ears.

14. When clay is leather-hard, smooth surface with a damp sponge. Let the coal-pot dry thoroughly. Bake in the oven until hard. No glaze is needed.

CHINESE CANDLE HOLDER

In China, art objects—pottery, metalwork, painting, and furniture—are known by the dynasty in which they were made. Sung pottery was made during the Sung Dynasty, 960-1280 A.D. This cup is a copy of a stem cup which was probably made around 1100 A.D. in the province of Honan. Pottery from this section of China was covered with a clear olive-green glaze. Some of the potteries also turned out a glaze that was brownish green, and others a dull green-blue. The color formulas have since been lost, and no one has made "Sung" color again. These cups were used to hold liquids for drinking, but in this project the design has been used for a candle holder.

Materials and Tools
3½-pound box of oven-baked clay
glass dessert dish with flared edge—
   2 inches high, 5 inches in diameter
small juice glass or narrow jar
short thick candle
air-dried glazes or acrylic paints—
   green, brown, and white
clay-working tools
string—12-inch length
flat watercolor brush—¾ inch wide
   (Note: use a nylon brush for acrylic paint)

Directions
1. To know how large a clay slab you will need, measure the glass dessert dish. Turn the dish upside down. Hold a piece of string at the bottom edge. Bring the rest of the string up the side, over the top, and down the other side. Mark this end with the thumb and first finger of the other hand. Lay the string on a ruler. This measurement will give you the length and width of the slab of clay.
2. Roll out the slab of clay ¼ inch thick (using two ¼-inch lathes as guides), and about ½ inch larger in each direction than the measurement taken in Step 1.
3. When the clay is stiff enough to handle, but still soft enough to drape over the glass mold, lift up the slab. Place slab evenly over the bottom of the upside-down glass dessert dish. Transfer dish and slab to the top of the juice glass or narrow, straight-sided jar. Gently mold the clay against the dish, smoothing out any wrinkles or folds.

Trim off extra clay to the edge of the glass dish. (See drawings for Cameroon Grain Container, pages 17 and 18, Steps 3 and 4.)

4. Let the clay dry until it is stiff enough to hold its shape. Remove it from the glass bowl and place it upright on the plastic sheet surface. If it becomes too dry, you will not be able to take the clay off the mold, as it will have shrunk against the glass.

5. While the clay dries on the bowl, roll out a solid cylinder of clay, 1½ inches long and 1⅛ inches in diameter. Add a strip of clay, ½ inch wide and ⅛ inch thick, around the outside of one end of the cylinder. Smooth it into the cylinder at the top of the strip, and flare out the end (see drawing). Cut each end so the surface is flat. Let the roll dry a bit, then cut out a deep foot.

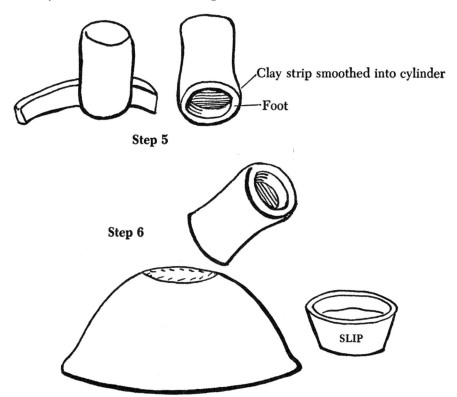

Clay strip smoothed into cylinder

Foot

Step 5

Step 6

SLIP

6. Mix about a tablespoon of slip. Attach small end of roll to the bottom of the clay bowl, using the slip. Let dry until leather-hard.

7. Smooth all surfaces with a damp sponge. Thin the edge of the bowl with a knife and the damp sponge.

8. Let the bowl and "stem" dry. The stem must dry all the way through; otherwise it will split when placed in the heat of the oven. It will take longer to dry than the bowl.
9. Bake in the oven.
10. Mix glazes and apply according to the manufacturer's directions. Or mix acrylic colors together to make a soft green with a little brown in it. Apply to the pottery stem cup with the ¾-inch brush. Let the stem cup stand undisturbed until the glaze or paint is hard dry. Then put the candle in the cup part, heating the bottom of the candle first so it will stick in place.

EGYPTIAN SCARAB

The ancient Egyptian scarab was a beetle design, symbolizing eternal life. It was made of baked and glazed clay, or carved from semi-precious stones. This scarab is made of clay glazed a bright blue-green, a favorite glaze color in ancient Egypt. It is worn as a pendant; small scarabs are often worn as ring ornaments.

Materials and Tools
1 sheet of typewriter paper
clear plastic wrap—8 x 12 inches
cellophane tape
1 tablespoon of oven-baked clay
acrylic paints—blue-green and white
nylon cord—1 yard maximum amount
clay-working tools
thin nail
round nylon brush—#3

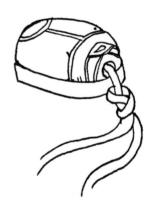

Directions
1. Copy the pattern of the scarab design on the piece of typewriter paper, using the grid method. Place the paper on a flat surface. Cover the paper with the clear plastic wrap held in place with cellophane tape.

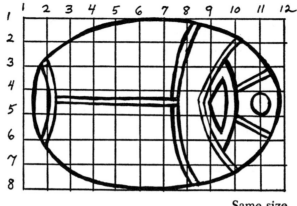

Same size

2. Scoop out a heaping tablespoon of clay from the box. Put the clay on the plastic-covered sheet of paper, in the middle of the scarab design.

3. Squeeze and mold the clay until the bottom of the lump fits the outline drawn on the typewriter paper. Scrape and smooth the clay until the sides slant upward and the top is gently rounded. The scarab should be about 1 to 1⅛ inch high (see drawing).

4. Mark the scarab design on the top of the clay shape, using the thin nail. Also make a small hole with the nail at the head of the scarab, so it can be hung on a cord.

5. Let the scarab dry until leather-hard. Smooth lightly with a damp sponge. Turn the scarab over and draw a design with the nail on the flat surface or carve your initials in the clay.

6. Let the clay dry thoroughly, then bake in the oven.

7. When the scarab is baked and cool, mix the acrylic paint. Add a little white paint to the blue-green color to soften it. Paint top and sides. Let dry, then turn the scarab over and paint the bottom. Let dry.

8. Run the cord through the hole at the top of the scarab. Tie a knot in the cord at the top edge of the scarab. Bring the cord around your neck and tie a bow at the back to hold the cord in place.

ENGLISH TOBY JUG

Toby jugs were first made by a Staffordshire potter around 1765, and have been popular ever since. Originally these brightly-colored jugs were sold at fairs. Used as decorations, as well as useful cream jugs, they were humorous figures—soldiers, or farmers, or portraits of famous men. Toby jugs are still made in England and shipped all over the world, but now they are manufactured, instead of being made by hand.

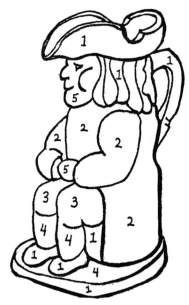

Color Key:
1 = black
2 = red
3 = blue
4 = white
5 = pink (red + white)

Face:
Lips and cheeks: red
Eyes: blue
Eyebrows and eye outlines: black

Materials and Tools
3½-pound box of oven-baked clay
straight-sided jelly or drinking glass—
　3 to 4 inches high
1 sheet of typewriter paper
acrylic paints—white, black, blue and red
acrylic polymer gloss medium
compass
clay-working tools
flat nylon brush—¾ inch wide
round nylon brushes—#2 and #5

Directions

1. Roll out a ¼-inch thick slab of clay, using two strips of ¼-inch wood lathe as guides for the rolling pin. Cut a strip of clay with the knife, as wide as the glass is high, and long enough to wrap around the glass.

2. Wrap clay around the wet glass, and seal the two ends with slip. Smooth the surface so the joining does not show. Let dry a little.

3. Measure the diameter of the bottom of the glass; on the typewriter paper, draw a circle with the compass, ½ inch larger in diameter than the bottom of the glass. Add a straight area on one side, ½ inch wide in the center (see drawing). This will stick out at the front of the jug as a foot rest. Cut out the pattern with scissors.

4. Place the paper pattern on the slab of clay and cut out around the edges with the knife. Set clay aside until stiff enough to handle.

5. Cut a second strip of clay, 1¼ inches wide, and long enough to fit around the top of the glass. Cut the two short edges at a 45° angle. Set aside until stiff enough to handle, but not so stiff that it cannot be formed into a circle.

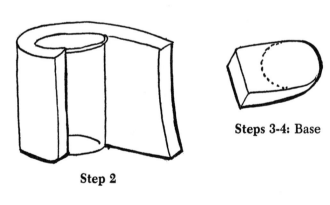

Steps 3-4: Base

Step 2

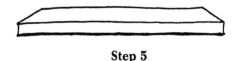

Step 5

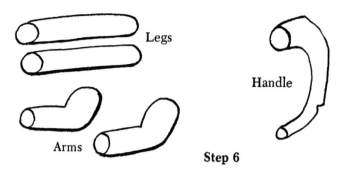

Legs

Handle

Arms

Step 6

6. Make two small rolls of clay, 1½ inches long and ½ inch in diameter, for the legs. Make another roll, 1½ inches long and ½ inch in diameter, and cut it in half lengthwise for the two arms. The final roll of clay is 4 to 5 inches long and ¾ inch in diameter, flattened slightly for the handle. Curve it into the shape of the handle, according to the drawing. Set aside all rolls to stiffen a bit, but not so much that they cannot be bent.

7. When the clay around the glass has dried enough to stand alone, remove it from the glass. Smear the bottom edge of the cylinder with slip. Add a line of slip around the top edge of the circle part of the bottom addition, scratching the clay around the circle. Put the clay cylinder over the circle and smooth the joint with slip. The ½-inch shelf will stick out from the cylinder, and this area will be the front of the jug.

8. Add the two legs to the front of the cylinder, holding them in place with slip. Make two ½-inch rolls of clay for the feet; add them to the bottom of the legs, so they rest on the shelf of clay.

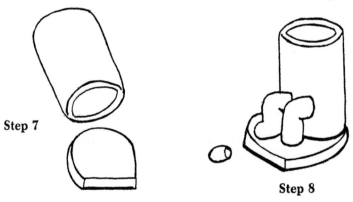

Step 7

Step 8

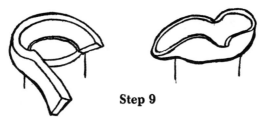

Step 9

9. The flared top and lip of the pitcher form the hat of the Toby jug soldier. Add the 1¼-inch strip of clay to the top of the cylinder of clay, holding it in place with slip. Bring the two short edges together at the back of the cylinder and hold with slip, smoothing the joint. Gently flare out this top strip, forming it in front into a pinched pouring lip. Also slightly flare out each side into a point so that this top strip looks like a tricorn hat.

10. Add the curved handle to the back of the jug opposite the front lip, using slip to attach it.

Squeeze for waistline

Steps 10-11

11. Now for the last additions to the jug. Add the two half-roll arms on each side of the cylinder, bending them halfway down into an angle and attaching them with slip. Add extra clay to the end of each arm, pressing it flat into hands that meet over the knees. Add a beaked nose in front, using slip to attach it to the cylinder, and add hair at the sides and back of the head. Also form the eyes, mouth, cheeks, and chin, modeling them with your fingers and the point of the knife. Cut a foot in the flat bottom.

12. As the clay dries, smooth any rough edges with a damp sponge. Let dry thoroughly, and sandpaper any areas that need it when the surface is totally dry.

13. Bake the Toby jug in the oven. When finished, take out and let cool.

14. Paint the jug with acrylic colors, following the color notes on the drawing on page 28. Paint the inside with white acrylic. Use the ¾-inch flat brush for large areas, and the #2 and #5 round brushes to paint the smaller areas.

15. When paint is dry, cover the whole surface, inside and out, with acrylic polymer gloss medium, using the ¾-inch flat nylon brush, and let the coating dry.

JAPANESE WIND CHIMES

Japanese gardens are small affairs, landscapes in miniature. Each part is chosen and placed with care—rocks, individual trees, gravel, water, and green areas. Wind chimes are hung on a tree branch or from a porch or door beam, giving sound to the wind. Even the slightest breeze sets the chimes in motion, filling the air with low, gentle tones; strong winds will blow the clay disks against each other with a banging, clashing noise.

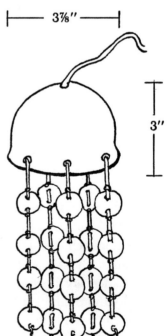

Materials and Tools
3½-pound box of oven-baked clay
1 sheet of typewriter paper
nylon fishing line—60-inch length
heavy twine—18-inch length
acrylic polymer gloss medium
compass
oven-proof ramekin—3⅜ inches in
    diameter, 2¾ inches high
clay-working tools
thin 2-inch nail
flat nylon brush—¾ inch wide
toothpicks

Directions

1. Using the compass, draw two circles on the typewriter paper, one 8½ inches in diameter, the other 1 inch in diameter. Cut out both circles with scissors.

2. Roll out a ¼-inch thick slab of clay, using ¼-inch wood lathes, and use the paper pattern to cut out an 8½-inch circle.

3. Turn the ramekin upside down. Moisten the sides, then drape the circle of clay over the ramekin. Gently smooth out any wrinkles or creases. Cut away extra clay around the open edge of the ramekin. Set aside to dry a little. (See drawings, Cameroon Grain Container, pages 17 and 18, Steps 3 and 4.)

4. Lay the 1-inch circle pattern on top of the clay slab, and cut around the edge with the point of the knife. Repeat until you have 20 circles. Pull away the extra clay from between the circles, and let the circles dry a bit.

Step 4

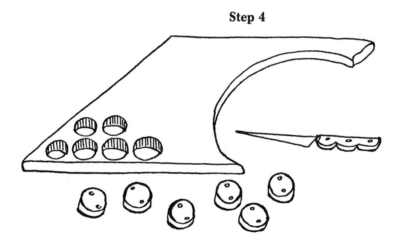

5. When the clay on the ramekin mold is dry enough to stand alone, ease it off the mold. Turn the clay pot upright. With your fingers and a damp sponge, smooth and thin the edge; at the same time slightly curve ½ inch of the rim outward into a flared edge. With a thin nail, make five evenly spaced holes ½ inch in from the edge. Smooth the clay around the holes. Make a larger hole in the center of the top. Let dry resting on the top.

6. Smooth both surfaces and edges of all the circles, using the damp sponge. With the thin nail, put two holes through each circle—one above the other—each one ¼ inch in from the edge.

7. After the pot and the circles are dry, bake them in the oven.

8. When baked and cooled, cover all surfaces with two coats of acrylic polymer gloss medium, allowing the first coat to dry before adding the second. Be sure that the holes do not fill up with the liquid. Poke a toothpick through each one to clear out any liquid.

9. Cut the nylon fishing line into five 12-inch lengths. String four circles on one length of fishing line, tying knots at each hole to keep the circles in position. The circles should be ¾ inch apart. Repeat with all the circles, until all five lengths of fishing line are used up.

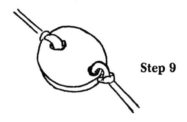

Step 9

10. Tie each strip to a hole in the edge of the pot. Adjust the line to the length you want. Make a large knot in one end of the heavy twine. String it through the top hole in the pot, with the knot inside the pot.

11. Hang the wind chimes where the breeze will blow gently through them, making the circles clash together.

Variation: The circles can be tied in irregular numbers on different lengths of nylon line, but be sure that there are enough circles opposite each other to clash together.

PUERTO RICAN SUNBURST TILE

Because of Puerto Rico's close ties to Spain in the early days, the local craftspeople made tiles for floor and wall coverings. These tile designs were often copies of Spanish designs. However, in this

Enlarge to ½″ squares

project, a modern Puerto Rican tile design has been used: a tropical sun carved deeply into the clay and covered with a single, soft color, rather than the more elaborate Spanish designs.

Materials and Tools
1 sheet of typewriter paper
3½-pound box of oven-baked clay
acrylic paints or air-dried glazes—white and soft green
compass
pointed spoon
clayworking tools
flat watercolor brush—¾ inch wide
(Note: use a nylon brush for acrylic paint)

Directions
1. With the compass, draw a 5-inch circle on the typewriter paper. Enlarge the pattern design to fit the circle, using the grid method. Cut out the circle with scissors.

2. Roll out a slab of clay, ½ inch thick and 6 inches square, using ½-inch wood lathes.

3. Place the paper pattern on top of the clay slab. Cut around the edge of the pattern with a sharp knife. Remove excess clay from around the circle and put it back into the box. Follow the design pattern with a sharp pencil, so that the lines are pressed into the clay surface.

4. With the pointed spoon, scoop out a $3/16$- to $1/4$-inch wide line, $1/8$ inch deep, all around each flame-like shape (see drawing). Let dry.

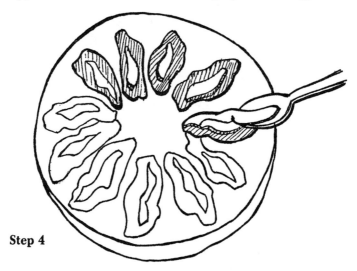

Step 4

5. When clay is leather-hard, remove any crumbles of clay from the scooped-out design. Then smooth the surface with a damp sponge. Let the clay dry completely before baking.

6. Bake the clay tile in the oven.

7. When clay is baked, let it cool. The color for the tile is a soft gray-green, made by mixing a little green in the white; use either acrylic paint or air-dried glaze. Apply the color to the top of the tile, and let dry. The color will pull away from the edges of the scooped-out design, showing the rust color clay underneath. If it does not, rub away a line of paint or glaze around the edges of the design; use a piece of face tissue, wrapped around your forefinger, to remove the not-quite-dry paint or glaze.

SPANISH TILE

The art of brightly painted, glazed tiles was brought to Spain by the Moors when they conquered the southern part of the country. Tiles were used decoratively to cover walls and floors of buildings, both inside and out, as wood had been scarce in North Africa. Even today the use of tiles on floors persists in the countries around the Mediterranean Sea.

The design for this project is copied from tiles on the walls of the Alhambra in Granada, which was built by the Moors in the fourteenth century. It was at the Alhambra, in 1492, that Ferdinand and Isabella met with Columbus. After listening to his plans, they agreed to send him on his voyage westward across the Atlantic Ocean to the Indies.

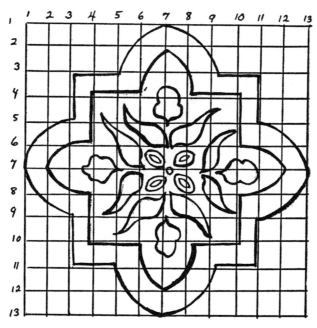

Enlarge to ½″ squares

Materials and Tools
3½-pound box of oven-baked clay
1 sheet of typewriter paper
1 sheet of graphite paper
air-dried glazes or acrylic paints—
   dark red, dark blue, and white
clay-working tools
round watercolor brushes—#3 and #8
flat watercolor brush—¾ inch wide
   (Note: use nylon brushes for acrylic paints)

Directions
1. Roll out a ½-inch thick slab of clay, using ½-inch wood lathes. Measure a 6-inch square of clay, and cut with a sharp-pointed knife. Let the clay dry a bit before moving it. Return extra clay, well-wrapped in plastic, to the box to be used for another project.
2. While the clay is drying, enlarge the pattern of the tile design by the grid method on the sheet of typewriter paper.
3. When the clay square is leather-hard, smooth the top surface and sides. Then turn the square over and cut a foot in the bottom (see page 14).
4. When the clay square is totally dry, place it in the oven to bake.
5. After the square tile has been baked and cooled, transfer the design to the surface with graphite paper.
6. Paint the colored design with air-dried glazes or acrylic paints on

Color Key:
1 = white
2 = dark red
3 = dark blue

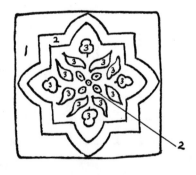

Step 6

the top surface of the tile. Use the ¾-inch flat brush for the background, and round brushes for design. Follow color directions on the pattern.

7. Allow the colored design to dry. Place tile on a table or on the wall as a decoration.

Fabric Folk Arts

Techniques of Working with Fabric

Cutting out fabric

Pin the enlarged paper pattern to the cloth or other material. If you are only cutting a single piece, pin the pattern to the right side of the cloth or material. If you are cutting two pieces of the same pattern which are to be seamed together, fold the fabric in half with the right sides facing each other. The pattern is pinned through both thicknesses on the wrong side of the fabric. Cut through the two layers of cloth along the edges of the pattern. Remove pins and pattern. Do not separate the two pieces of cloth.

Sewing a strengthened seam

With a ruler, measure the seam width shown on the pattern with right sides of the fabric together. Pin the two thicknesses of fabric together on the seam line. Thread the needle with the matching thread, and make a knot at the free end.

Sew small stitches all along the seam line, removing the pins as you stitch. When you reach the end, tie off the thread with several stitches in the same place. Loop the thread through itself to make a small knot. Now strengthen the seam by sewing over the same line, but reverse the position of the running stitches. The needle and thread will go under the stitch that shows on the surface, then over the unstitched space. This will make a solid line of stitching.

If the project is a double-sided object that is to be stuffed, then

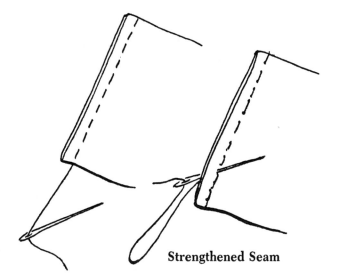

Strengthened Seam

leave an opening in the seam as shown on the pattern. Turn the project inside out; the seam will be on the inside, and the right side of the material will be showing.

Optional: If you are allowed to use the sewing machine, use it for the seams, or ask an adult to sew the seams for you.

Gathering

To gather material, make tiny running stitches with needle and thread. Make three rows of stitches, the first row being ⅛ inch from the edge of the material, the rest ⅛ inch apart. When you have finished a row, leave about 4 inches of thread at the end of the stitching; cut the thread and tie a knot in the end. When all three

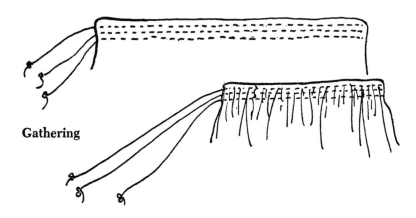

Gathering

rows have been stitched, gently ease the material along the stitches, while holding on to the extra length of threads. Pull the material as tight as you need to. Tie the extra threads together and cut off the excess thread.

Blind-stitching

Blind-stitching is used to close an opening after stuffing an object, such as the Appalachian doll or the Indian camel. Turn under the seam material on each side of the opening, holding it in place with pins. Sew the opening together by putting the needle and thread through the folded edge—first one side, then the other. Pull the sides toward each other so they just meet, as you sew along the opening. Finish off the end with an over-and-under stitch, looping the thread through the last stitch. Cut off the excess thread.

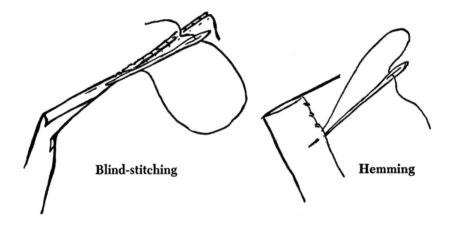

Blind-stitching   **Hemming**

Hemming

For narrow hems, turn the edge of the fabric twice over on itself on the wrong side, and pin in position. Thread the needle and put a knot in the other end of the thread. Take small, angled stitches around the edge of the hem, taking up a bit of the base fabric and a bit of the folded edge of the hem with the needle point. Pull the thread through, and then make the next stitch. Try not to take too much of the base fabric, as then the stitches will show on the right side.

Overhand Stitching

Overhand stitching

This is sometimes called *whipping*. The overhand stitch is used to hold two pieces of fabric together with a very narrow seam along their edges.

The edges of the two pieces of fabric are placed together, right sides facing each other. The overhand stitch goes through the two pieces of fabric, just in from their edges, then over the top edges, then back again through the fabric. This prevents the fabric from fraying, which is very useful when working with loosely woven materials. The stitch is also used for non-fraying, heavy fabrics such as felt or heavy plastic to reduce a bulky seam. With these fabrics the seam is often placed on the right side of the fabric as a decorative feature.

French knot

For French knots, use a large-eyed embroidery needle. Thread the needle with *embroidery thread* or *floss*, in the color shown on the design pattern. Put a knot in the free end.

Pull the full length of thread through the cloth, from back to front, at one of the pattern dots on the material. Hold the thread straight up with the other hand, thumb and forefinger grasping the thread about 2 to 3 inches above the cloth. Put the needle against the thread, just above the cloth level, with the thread touching the needle about ½ *inch above its point*. Now, move the needle point four or five times in tiny circles around the tightly drawn thread, taking up part of the 2 to 3 inches of tautly held thread. The thread must be wrapped closely around the needle. Then, without loosening the circles of thread or releasing the held length, push the point

French Knot

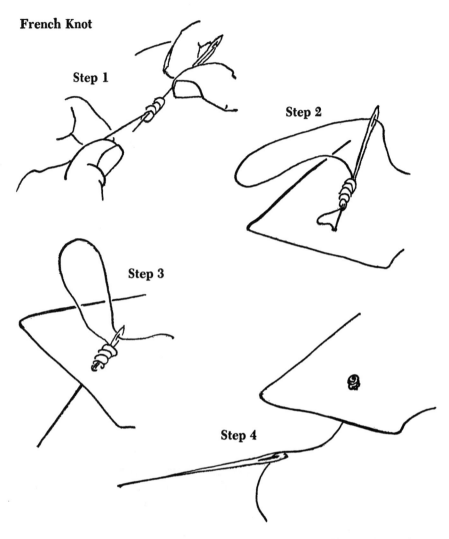

Step 1

Step 2

Step 3

Step 4

of the needle through the cloth, right beside the place where the thread was pushed up through the cloth. *Do not* push the needle and thread through the same hole again. Slowly pull the needle through the cloth to the wrong side, still holding the excess thread with the other hand. The thread will be pulled through the circles of thread, forming a knot on the surface of the cloth.

Bring the needle over to the next dot, push it up to the right side, and repeat the circling and knotting.

Do all the knots of the one color at one time, as shown on the design, then change the thread to another color. Go on to the next set of knots; repeat until the design is complete.

AFRICAN INDIGO CLOTH

For thousands of years, indigo has been the main coloring dye for cotton fabric. All over Africa, a blue dye has been made from the leaves of the indigo plant. The plant and the preparation of the dye were brought to Africa from India. From Africa it came to the Americas, and fields of indigo were planted in the southern United States. This was the original dye used for overalls, jeans, and any dark blue fabric color.

In Africa, the dye was also used to form decorative patterns on white cotton fabric. In Ghana the combed pattern was popular. Often a printed pattern was added as part of the decoration. The patterns were cut from hard-dried calabash (squash) rinds in designs of birds, animals, fishes, leaves, or flowers. In this project the leaf design is cut from styrofoam; the blue color is made with cold-water dye and the printed design with blue acrylic paint.

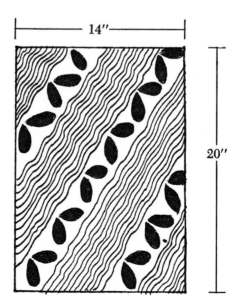

Materials and Tools
unbleached muslin or white sheeting—15 x 21 inches
white sewing thread
1 box cold-water fabric dye—light blue
balsa wood—2 x 3 x ⅛ inches
small can of white shellac
1 sheet of typewriter paper
styrofoam—2 x 3 x 1¼ inches (from dime store
  or from packaging of fragile items)
clear plastic wrap—6 inches square
ball of absorbent cotton—1¼ inches in diameter
acrylic paint—bright or dark blue
pins
needle
scissors
string
electric iron
craft knife or craft saw
pencil
flat nylon brush—¾ inch wide
masking tape
lots of newspapers
shallow plastic dish for paint—4 inches wide
plastic spoon
flat plastic coffee can cover
2 thumbtacks

Directions
1. Make a ¼-inch hem around the edges of the unbleached muslin or cotton sheeting material.
2. Dye the fabric with the light blue cold-water dye. Follow manufacturer's directions on the package. Hang up to dry. When dry, iron out all the wrinkles; ask an adult to help you use the iron.
3. While the fabric is drying, cut out the comb from the balsa wood with the craft knife or saw. Follow measurements on the diagram before cutting the wood with the knife. Paint comb with two coats of shellac, using the ¾-inch brush.

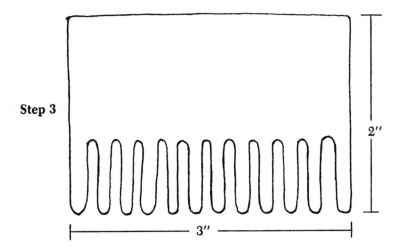

Step 3

2"

3"

4. Copy the leaf pattern by the grid method on the sheet of type-writer paper. Cut out the pattern with scissors, all around the outline. Lay the pattern on the styrofoam block and trace around the leaf edges with the pencil.

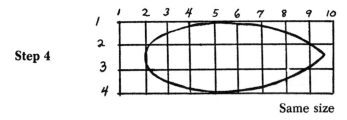

Step 4

Same size

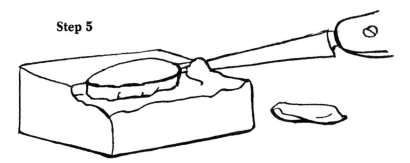

Step 5

5. Cut out the leaf pattern from the styrofoam with the craft knife.
6. When the fabric has been ironed, and the comb and printing block cut, fix a working surface. Put ten or twelve sheets of news-

paper flat on the working surface. Place the blue-dyed cloth on top of the newspapers, right side up. Hold it to the newspapers with the masking tape.

7. Mix 3 inches of blue acrylic paint with water in the shallow bowl. Check for the proper thinness by dipping the points of the wooden comb in the paint, then drawing the comb over a piece of extra fabric. Adjust if necessary with more paint or water.

8. When paint is the right thinness, dip the points of the comb into the paint. Draw wavy lines at an angle across the taped-down fabric (see drawing on page 45).

9. When all the angled lines have been added to the fabric, let it dry.

Step 10

10. Make a dabber, which is used to transfer the paint from the dish to the leaf pattern on the styrofoam block. Spread the piece of plastic food wrap on a flat surface. Place the wad of cotton in the center, flattening it a bit. Pull the sides of the wrap up around the cotton, and tie the wrap with a piece of string or thread close to the top of the wad of cotton. Flatten the bottom, and your dabber is complete.

11. Stir more paint and water together with the plastic spoon on the flat plastic coffee can top. Press dabber into the paint, then dab at the styrofoam printing block with an up-and-down motion. When the styrofoam leaf is covered with a thin coat of paint, turn the block over and press the leaf down on the fabric. Repeat the pattern until all the areas shown on the drawing are covered.

12. Let the fabric dry. Hang it on the wall, using thumbtacks.

Variation: When hemming the edges, make the top and bottom hems wide enough to hold a ½-inch diameter dowel (4 inches longer than the fabric). Run the dowels through the top and bottom hems to add weight to the wall hanging. Attach the ends of a length of cord to each end of the top dowel. Hang the fabric on the wall by the cord.

APPALACHIAN DOLL

In the Appalachian Mountains, from Virginia to Tennessee, the making of rag dolls for children has been a craft going back to the early settlers. In this mountain area one can still find the same products that the early settlers made and used. The craftspeople keep alive the old crafts of basket making, woodworking, furniture making, quilting, weaving, and pottery making. Children in the mountains still play with rag dolls. Here, in this project, is a doll dressed in gingham with hair of yarn, though it is stuffed with a modern product, polyester fiber.

Materials and Tools
brown wrapping paper
gingham patterned cloth—¼ yard
white cotton cloth or sheeting—5 x 12 inches
white sewing thread
polyester fiber filling—1-pound bag
2-ply yarn—a 2-ounce hank in black or yellow
ribbon to match color of gingham pattern—
   ¾ inches wide, 10 inches long
white household glue
pencil
ruler
scissors
pins
needle
1 sheet of graphite paper
measuring spoons
felt-tipped marking pens—black and red
small dish

10½"

Gingham Fabric

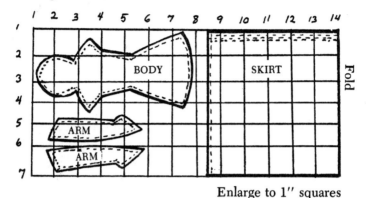

Enlarge to 1″ squares

White Fabric

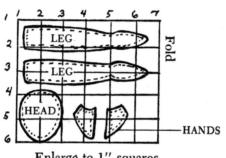

Enlarge to 1″ squares

Directions

1. Enlarge the patterns by the grid method on the sheet of wrapping paper. Cut out the patterns with the scissors.

2. On the long side of the gingham fabric, measure and cut a 26 x 6-inch piece. Fold the piece in half, right sides together, so that it measures 6 x 13 inches. Pin the patterns to the cloth, and cut out the separate pieces. You will have two of each piece. Do the same with the white fabric. With right sides together, sew each set of matching pieces together for body, arms, and legs. Make ¼-inch strengthened seams. Leave the top ends of the arms and legs and the bottom of the body open, without a seam.

3. Turn each piece right side out. Stuff with polyester fiber filling.

4. Turn under the open seams of the arms, legs, and body, and blind-stitch them together.

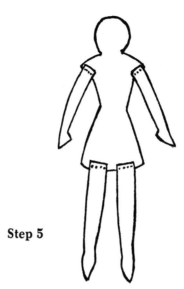

Step 5

5. Sew arms to the upper sides of the body. Sew legs to the bottom edge of the body. Add shoes with black felt-tipped pen.

6. To make the skirt, open the folded rectangle of gingham; it will measure 11 x 6 inches. Turn the fabric over to the wrong side and pin down a ½-inch hem along one long edge. Sew in place with a hemming stitch. Sew two lines of small running stitches along the other long edge.

7. Fold the skirt material in half, right sides together, matching the two short sides. Sew the short sides together with a ¼-inch seam. Turn skirt right side out.

8. Pull the tube of material over the legs and body of the doll, the hem at the bottom. Gather the skirt around the waist by pulling the threads of the running stitches. Tie the two threads of the running stitches into a knot when the skirt fits tightly at the waist. Tack skirt to waist with a few stitches in four places.

9. Tie the ribbon around the waist to cover the top edge of the skirt and the gathers. Make a bow in the back.

10. On one of the white cloth ovals, use graphite paper to transfer the eyebrows, eyes, nose, and mouth. Also transfer the hair guidelines. Trace over the graphite lines of all but the mouth with

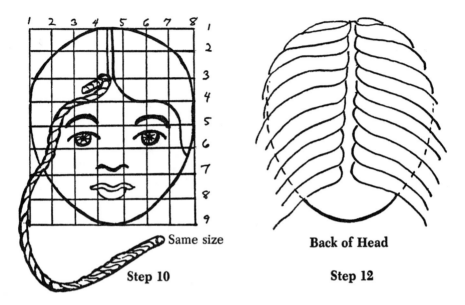

Same size

Step 10

Back of Head

Step 12

the black felt-tipped marking pen. Fill in the mouth with the red felt-tipped marking pen.

11. Blind-stitch the face to the front of the head, turning raw edges in around the seam and bottom edge of face. Repeat with back of head.

12. For the hair, cut yarn into 4½-inch lengths. Put 2 teaspoons of white glue into a small dish, add ½ teaspoon water, and stir. Starting at one of the lowest graphite lines on the front of the face near the eyes, glue the yarn to the cloth. Dip ¼ inch of one end of a length of yarn in the glue. Press the glued end of the yarn on the graphite line nearest the eye. Repeat with strips of yarn to cover the full length of the line, holding the yarn outward and slightly down as shown in the drawing. Let dry, and start the next line. When you come to the center part, the direction of the pieces of yarn is reversed. This is so that the ends of the yarn will be covered when you pull back the hair. Repeat on the back of the head.

13. When all the yarn is attached and the glue is dry, bring the yarn to the back of the neck. Twist around into a large knot and sew in place. Or bring each half of the yarn to the side, and tie near the head into pigtails.

14. The final step is to make the two hands. Place the right sides of two hand shapes together. Sew a ⅛-inch seam around the curved edge—leave the straight edge open. Turn inside out. Repeat with the other two pieces. Pull the hands over the end of each arm. Turn under the edges, and blind-stitch to the arms.

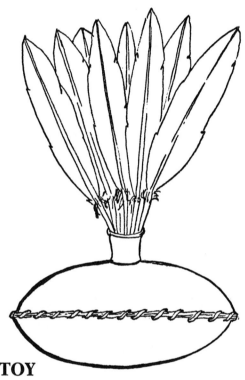

BRAZILIAN PETECA TOY

In Brazil, an ancient game is still played. The "ball" is like a shuttlecock, only larger, approximately 12 inches high, and is called a *peteca*. It is made of leather and the wing or tail feathers of a large bird. The *peteca* is kept in the air by upward batting with the palm of the hand on the flat, round bottom of the stuffed leather circle. It goes back and forth among the players who try to keep it in the air. This project substitutes naugahyde, a plastic, leather-like material, for the original leather, and uses barred wing feathers bought at a craft store or by mail order.

Materials and Tools
1 sheet of typewriter paper
black or brown naugahyde—7¾ x 10½ inches
wood glue, 2-tube epoxy cement, or contact cement
1 spool heavy button and carpet thread,
   or 5 feet of thin vinyl or suede lacing thread
   or lacing to match color of naugahyde
polyester fiber filling—large handful
7 or 8 dark barred wing feathers—10 to 12 inches long
compass
pencil
ruler
scissors
round watercolor brush—#3
thin sharp nail or awl
hammer
heavy needle
masking tape
2 paper clips

Directions
1. With the compass, draw two circles, 5 inches in diameter, on the typewriter paper. Cut out the circles with the scissors. Place circles on the naugahyde, and cut out. Also cut out a 2¼ x 2½-inch piece of naugahyde.
2. Use the hammer to make matching holes with the thin sharp nail, awl, or other punch-like pointed tool, along the edge of the top and bottom circles, ⅜ inch apart. Draw a ¾-inch diameter circle in the middle of one of the 5-inch circles. Cut out with the scissors.
3. Roll the small piece of naugahyde into a tube, 2¼ inches long. Overlap the edges ¼ inch, add glue with the #3 brush, and squeeze edges together. Follow the manufacturer's directions for gluing. Hold the seam together with two paper clips, top and bottom, until the glue is dry. When the seam is dry, make cuts all around one end of the tube. They should be ¼ inch apart and ⅜ inch deep.
4. Cover the inside edges around the small circle opening in the 5-inch circle with glue, using the #3 brush. Put the tube through

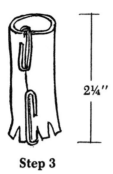

Step 3

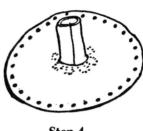

Step 4

the hole from front to back. Flatten out the ¼-inch wide cut pieces at the edge of the tube against the glued surface. Press down on the outside of the large circle, so that tube and circle will be glued together. Let dry completely.

5. Sew the edges of the two 5-inch circles together with the heavy carpet thread or plastic lacing. Pull the cord or lacing through the holes. Leave 2 inches unsewn, but do not cut the thread or lacing.

6. Stuff the polyester fiber filling through the 2-inch opening, until the inside is completely stuffed and hard. Finish sewing up the opening.

7. Bunch the feathers together. Paint the quills at the bottom with glue. Hold the quills and glue together in a solid mass, by wrapping them with the masking tape around the lower 2 inches of the quills. When the glue has hardened, paint the outside of the masking tape with glue, and slip into the upright tube of naugahyde. Squeeze the outside of the tube with one hand until the glue is set, then let dry until hard.

FRENCH KNOT PICTURES

An old embroidery stitch called a French knot is used for these pictures. This is a stitch which forms small knots of thread all over the surface of the fabric. The knots can be close together or far apart. (See page 43 for all directions.) The designs for these pictures are similar to those painted on old French plates.

Lamb: blue fabric;
black ear, eye, mouth, hooves

House: blue fabric

Rooster: white fabric;
black eye, beak, inner
comb outline, wing outline

Color Key:
1 = white
2 = red
3 = yellow
4 = green
Outlines: black

Materials and Tools
heavy cotton fabric—7 x 7-inch
   piece of white or plain color
matching sewing thread
1 sheet of typewriter paper
1 sheet of graphite paper
embroidery floss—white, black, red, yellow, and green
pencil
ruler
needle
scissors
dish towel
electric iron
glass-covered picture frame, same size as fabric;
   or heavy cardboard, double-sided tape, and
   clear plastic wrap

Directions

1. If you are embroidering the lamb, which will be covered with white knots, use a colored fabric for the background. Make your choice of colored fabric for other patterns, depending on the design colors.

2. Sew a narrow hem around the edges of the fabric.

3. Use the grid method to enlarge on the typewriter paper whichever pattern you choose. With graphite paper, transfer the pattern to the fabric with small dots instead of a solid line.

Enlarge to 1″ squares

4. Fill in the design and outline with French knots. Follow directions for colors as shown on the patterns.

5. When finished, press out all wrinkles with a moderately hot iron; ask an adult to help. Press on the wrong side over a dish towel that is folded several times into a pad. This will prevent the knots from being pressed flat.

6. Put the picture into a glass-covered frame. You can also tape the back to a piece of heavy cardboard with double-sided tape. Then cover embroidered side and cardboard back with clear plastic food wrap, held in place with tape.

HAWAIIAN SEED NECKLACE

All through the area of the Pacific and the Caribbean islands, local people have made necklaces and bracelets of seeds. Some of the seeds are brightly colored, others are light tan, brown, black, gray, or white. The seeds are often dyed with vegetable and root dyes. This necklace is a copy of one made in Hawaii. Cantaloupe seeds, colored with brown water dye, are used instead of the Hawaiian dark brown seeds. Beads replace the oval gray seeds.

Materials and Tools
seeds from several cantaloupes or other melons
5 to 7 brown, white, gray, or brightly colored beads—
    ¼ to ⅜ inch in diameter
1 package of dark brown water dye (Rit or Tintex)
nylon sewing thread, or 1 package bead-stringing thread
needle
2 plastic containers—4½ inches in diameter,
    3 inches deep, for dye
measuring cup
tablespoon
fine mesh sieve
scissors
felt-tipped pen
ruler
paper towels
newspapers

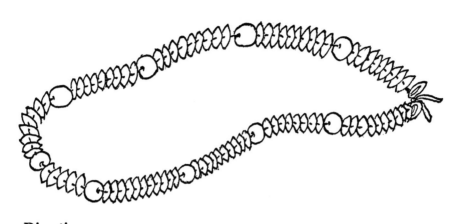

Directions

1. Remove seeds from cantaloupes or other melons, and put them into a sieve. Wash the seeds under running tap water, removing all pieces of melon fiber. When they are clean, spread seeds out on paper towels to dry. The dried seeds can be kept for several months before using.

2. Mix the dye bath in one of the plastic containers. Put 1 tablespoon of dark brown dye in the container. Add 2 tablespoons of hot water, and stir to melt the dye. Then pour ½ cup of hot water from the faucet into the dye and stir to mix. Add ⅓ cup of seeds. Stir well, and then let them soak in the dye for one hour. If you have more than ⅓ cup of seeds, increase the amount of dye and water.

3. When seeds are well colored, hold the sieve over the other plastic container, and pour out dye bath and seeds into the sieve. Pour dye bath directly down the drain so it will not stain the sink. Rinse seeds, starting with hot water and ending with cold water. When the water running through the seeds in the sieve is clear, turn seeds out on newspapers covered with paper toweling to dry.

4. Hold the nylon thread around your neck to measure how long the necklace will be. It should be long enough to go over your head. Add 2 inches of extra thread at each end, and cut off thread.

5. Bring ends together on a flat surface, and stretch out the two sides of the thread. Mark the center with the felt-tipped pen. Plan where you want to add the beads, and mark the thread with the felt-tipped pen. Also mark the thread 2 inches in from each end.

6. Thread the needle and tie a knot 2 inches in from the other end of the thread, at the pen mark. Push the needle through the flat center of each seed at the broadest point, pulling the thread through. Pull the seed down to the knot. Repeat with each seed. When you reach the pen mark, add a bead, then continue with seeds.

7. When you have filled the thread with seeds and beads and have reached the mark 2 inches from the end, remove the needle from the thread. Tie a knot at the 2-inch mark. Then tie the two ends together in a knot. Cut off the extra ends or tie the ends into a bow.

INDIAN FELT CAMEL

For years, craftspeople in India have made and sold stuffed and brilliantly decorated small camels, in sizes anywhere from five inches to over three feet. These are covered with brightly colored felt or other fabrics. They are decorated with felt, silk, or velvet; gold and colored cord; sequins, small mirrors, or jewels—or all three. In this project the small camel is covered with yellow felt, with a green felt hump and cap, and decorated with cord, sequins, tiny mirrors, and tassels—all of which can be bought at notions counters or trimming stores.

Materials and Tools

1 sheet of typewriter paper
yellow felt—¼ yard
sewing thread—yellow
white household glue
string
green felt—8 x 10-inch piece
gift wrapping cord—gold and red
package of assorted colored sequins
small mirror circles—½-inch diameter (optional)
10 to 12 small tassels—¾ inch long
twine—4-inch length
pencil
ruler
scissors
pins
needle
small plastic container for glue
flat watercolor brush—¾ inch wide
polyester fiber filling—1-pound bag

Directions

1. Enlarge the pattern and oval form on the typewriter paper, using the grid method. Cut out the patterns with the scissors.

2. Pin the camel pattern to the felt (see diagram). With the scissors, cut out the two halves of the camel. Cut out one oval piece. Remove the pattern.

3. Pin both sides of the camel together. The leg flaps are left unpinned. Insert and pin the oval piece to the belly area of the camel. Sew a narrow overhand seam all around, wherever there is a *broken* line on the diagram. *Do not sew* where the line is solid; these are the openings for the legs, the front of the neck, and one side of the belly.

4. After sewing the seams, put a thin line of white glue between each half of the seam, and press the felt together. When the glue is dry, turn the felt camel right side out.

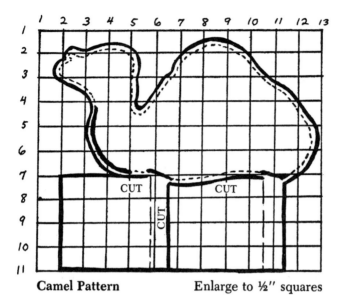

Camel Pattern   Enlarge to ½″ squares

Cut along heavy outline; inner line is seam line.

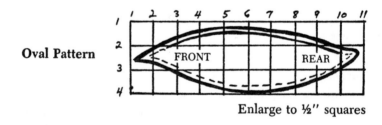

Oval Pattern   Enlarge to ½″ squares

Layout of Patterns on Felt

5. Next, form the legs. First mix a little water with the white glue in a small container. With the flat ¾-inch brush, lightly spread the glue over the inside (wrong side) surface of one of the rectangles for a front leg. Starting at the outside front end, roll the rectangle into a tight roll. Tie in three places with string until dry. At the upper edge of the roll, make ⅛-inch deep cuts, every ⅛ inch, around the outside cover of the felt, leaving the inside part of the roll of felt uncut. This cut area will be turned back, and then glued down on the inside of the camel. Repeat the gluing, spreading, rolling, tying, and cutting on the other three rectangles. Long broken lines on the pattern rectangles show the width of the legs.

6. When all the rolls are dry, cut and remove the strings. Put each leg through its opening in the bottom of the camel's body. Turn back the cut edges of felt at the top of each leg. Glue down the cut margin to the inside of the body. Hold in place with your fingers until the glue holds fast. Let dry thoroughly.

7. Next, stuff the camel with the polyester fiber filling. Poke the filling into the head, then fill the body until it is fat and hard. Sew up the neck and the belly seam with a blind stitch.

8. Test the camel for standing level, and trim off the bottom of the legs if they are uneven.

9. All the trimmings of the camel are put on with glue. Cut and add the green felt hump and cap. Do this by measuring directly on the camel. Follow the drawing for position. Trim the felt with gold and red cord. Add a halter of gold cord around the camel's nose, and let the cord hang loosely before attaching it to the front part of the hump. Hang tassels at each side of the cord around the neck. Tassels can also decorate the bottom of the hump. Add hoofs of the green felt to the legs. Paste the colored sequins and small mirrors all over the camel. Also form a solid circle of sequins at the top of the camel's hump. Finally, add a tail of the brown twine.

INDONESIAN BATIK SCARF

Batik is a Javanese word meaning "wax painting." The Javanese have always made designs for their clothing with a hot wax and boiled dye combination on cotton cloth. Beeswax was easily found in the hives of the wild bees in the forests. The dyes were made from roots and leaves: blue from the indigo plant; red from the root of the madder plant; yellow from the gummy sap of the mangosteen tree;

and brown from other tree barks mixed with the indigo blue to make a black dye.

For this project, a very simple batik process is used. It combines painted-on dyes and a washable paste wax which is applied with a brush or fingers. This process may be modern, but the design is a copy of an ancient Javanese sculpture, and the finished scarf looks like true batik.

Materials and Tools
lightweight, natural fiber, white cotton fabric—
    1 yard wide, ¼ yard long
white sewing thread
1 sheet of typewriter paper
1 sheet of graphite paper—18 x 24 inches (cut down to 9 x 13 inches)
masking tape
4 jars of cold-water dye or textile paint—
    magenta, turquoise blue, yellow, and brown
1 bottle of print-base thickener (if needed)
textile wax resist paste
needle
scissors
pencil
ruler
newspapers
round watercolor brush—#4 or #5
flat watercolor brush—¾ inch wide
individual foil mixing pans, cupcake size
face tissues
electric iron
supplies and tools for dye or paint and wax,
    depending on manufacturer's directions

Directions

1. Fold ¼ inch of fabric over on itself on all sides of the cotton material to make a ⅛-inch wide hem.

2. Wash the fabric; dry it; then press if wrinkled (ask an adult to help).

3. Enlarge and transfer the design to the cloth, using the grid method and the graphite paper. Put one design at each end of the scarf. The bottom of the design is 2 inches in from the edge of the scarf; the sides are evenly spaced.

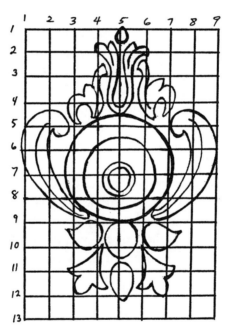

Enlarge to 1″ squares

4. Cover the working surface with several layers of newspaper. Change papers if they become soaked with paint.

5. Mix the textile paint or cold-water dye and print base according to the manufacturer's directions.

6. Paint the color on the fabric with a #4 or #5 brush, following the color notes on the drawing. Allow each color to dry before painting on the next color; otherwise the colors will run into each other. Or

Color Key:
1 = magenta red
2 = turquoise blue
3 = yellow
Outline: brown

you can leave a narrow line of unpainted fabric between each color. Put the color on a bit unevenly—it should not look like a perfectly printed design. When all the colors have been applied and are dry, outline the colored areas with brown. Let dry.

7. Spread the paste wax over the whole painted design, using the ¾-inch brush or your fingers. When the wax is dry, lightly crumple the fabric between your hands to make tiny crackle lines all over the wax surface.

8. *Thinly* brush the brown color over the wax so the paint sinks into the cracks. Blot the extra paint with wadded face tissues. Let dry. Be very careful that you do not drip any paint on the background fabric.

9. Wash out the wax, following the manufacturer's directions. Let the fabric dry, and then iron out the wrinkles.

ZULU WALL HANGING

The inside walls of Zulu huts were often decorated with small wall hangings made from unbleached or dyed cotton cloth. The cloth was decorated with sewn-on circles of hemp cord or other fiber cord, colored with vegetable dyes. Sometimes the circles were sewn together, then sewn to each other without a cotton cloth base. Here the base is blue burlap, very close in color to the indigo dye of Africa. The circles are made of 7-ply jute cord, in sun-gold and rust, and are glued to the burlap.

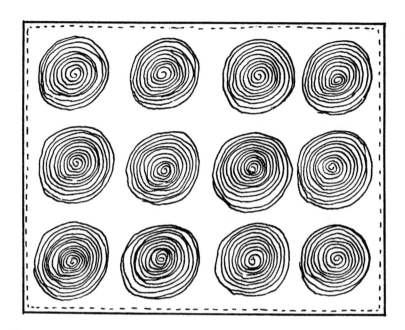

Materials and Tools
bright blue burlap—20 x 25 inches
matching blue sewing thread
1 sheet of typewriter paper
newspapers
masking tape
2 balls of 7-ply jute cord
   (198 feet to the ball)—sun-gold and rust
white household glue
ruler
compass
pencil
scissors
pins
needle
round watercolor brush—#3
chalk
long-shank, clear-top thumbtacks
wooden dowel—30 inches long, ½ inch in diameter (optional)
cord for hanging dowel—1 yard (optional)

Directions

1. Make a ¾-inch hem with a ¼-inch turn-under (1 inch of material in all) around all edges of the burlap. You can leave the two ends of the hem open on one long side. This will be the top of the wall hanging. The wooden dowel will go through the hem so the fabric can be hung on the wall with the cord.

2. Draw a 4-inch diameter circle with the compass on the typewriter paper. Cut out the circle with the scissors. This is the pattern for the jute cord circles. Slightly enlarge the hole in the center of the circle made by the compass point.

3. Put several sections of newspaper flat on the working surface. This should be in an area that can be left undisturbed for several days.

4. Place the hemmed piece of burlap on top of the newspapers, right side up. Smooth out the burlap and tape it along the edges to the newspapers.

5. The decoration for the burlap is formed of three rows of circles; each row has four circles, with 1 inch of space between each circle. There is a 2-inch margin all around the outside edge. With the ruler and chalk, measure the center of each circle (see drawing). Lay the pattern circle in position, placing the center hole over the chalk mark. Draw around the edge of the pattern circle with the chalk. Repeat with all the circles. If the chalk marks rub off as you work, re-measure and mark the burlap again with chalk.

6. Now start the first jute cord circle. Start in the upper left-hand corner with a rust circle. Paste down the free end of the cord at the center chalk mark. Bring the cord around the center in a tight circle, adding glue to the bottom of the cord, pressing the cord down against the burlap. If glue seems too thick, thin it a bit with water; always apply it with a fine-pointed brush. Add a little glue between the cords to hold them tightly together. Work slowly and carefully. When you get to the chalk circle outline, cut off the cord. Tuck the end under the last circle of cord, and glue it down. Put a book on top of the cord circle to hold it flat.

7. While the glue of the first circle is drying, start the second circle. If the book is in the way, work on another area of the burlap. Follow the drawing for color placement of the cord circles.

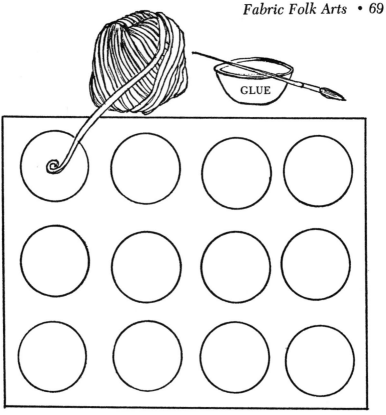

Steps 5-6

Color Key:
1 = rust
2 = gold

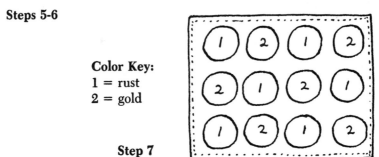

Step 7

8. Keeping adding circles of jute cord, following the color pattern, until the design is finished. Let everything dry thoroughly under the weight of books.

9. When dry, remove books and hang the burlap on a wall with the long thumbtacks. Or you can slip a wooden dowel through the top hem, and tie one end of a length of cord to each end of the dowel. Hang on the wall, using one of the long thumbtacks to hold the cord.

Gesso Folk Arts

❖ ❖ ❖

Techniques of Working with Gesso

Gesso powder is sold in art and craft stores. When mixed with water, it becomes a white, plaster-like material. Thick gesso has been used for centuries for raised designs on picture frames and boxes.

To make thick gesso, put 4 tablespoons of powder in a small bowl. Gradually add water, a half teaspoon at a time. Stir with a teaspoon until the mixture is smooth. Test a drop or two on a piece of aluminum foil. If it is thick enough to stand up without spreading, but thin enough to handle, you have the right thickness.

Next make a small cone of aluminum foil, about 3 or 4 inches long. Hold the side edge in place with cellophane tape. Cut a very small hole in the point of the cone with scissors. Put the gesso paste in the cone and fold the top over twice.

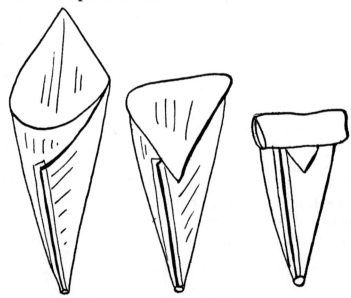

Hold the point of the cone just above the line of the design. Gently squeeze the cone from the top so the gesso drops down onto the pencil line in a steady flow. At the same time, move your hand and the cone in the direction of the line, always keeping the point of the cone just above the pencil line. Follow all the lines of the design with the gesso. You will end up with an overall pattern of raised lines.

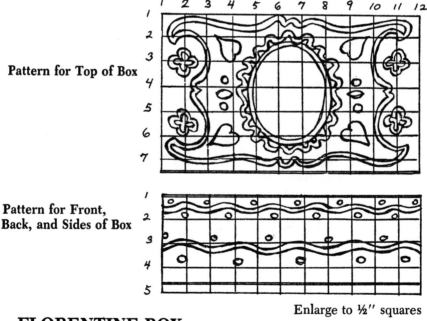

Pattern for Top of Box

Pattern for Front, Back, and Sides of Box

Enlarge to ½″ squares

FLORENTINE BOX

For generations, craftspeople in Florence, Italy, have decorated small wooden boxes with gesso. A small picture is painted on part of the box's lid, or a printed picture is pasted on the wood surface. Then the wood and the raised gesso decoration are covered with gilt paint or enamel. These small boxes were copies of more expensive gold boxes which were decorated with glass-enamel pictures.

Materials and Tools
wooden box—3⅛ x 5½ x 1⅞ inches
colored picture—2 x 1½ inches (approximately)
white household glue
face tissue
1 sheet of typewriter paper
1 sheet of graphite paper
gesso powder
white shellac
metallic hobby enamel—gold or brass
pencil
ruler
scissors
flat watercolor brush—¾ inch wide
round watercolor brush—#2
tools for preparing and applying gesso

Directions
1. Small wooden boxes with either a hinged or a removable lid can be bought in craft stores or by mail order. The small picture to be glued to the lid can be cut from a magazine or a postcard or greeting card, or it can be a color photograph. The shape can be square, rectangular, round, or oval. In cutting the picture to size, allow an extra ⅛ inch all around. This margin will be covered by the gesso as a frame.
2. With ruler and pencil, outline the picture's area in the center of the box lid.
3. With the #2 brush, apply white glue, thinned with a little water, within the pencil outline of the picture. Put the picture in place and smooth it by dabbing (not rubbing) the surface with a crumpled piece of face tissue. Let dry.

4. Enlarge the gesso design on the typewriter paper by the grid method, and transfer it to the top of the box with graphite paper. Allow for the size of your picture, and either shorten or lengthen the parts of the design near the picture. The design for the front, back, and sides of the box is a simple wavy line with dots at each curve. Draw this freehand, or enlarge and transfer it with graphite paper.

5. Paint all the surfaces of the box with shellac, using the ¾-inch brush. Cover the picture with a very thin coat of shellac, and do not brush over it after applying the shellac. Let dry. Then paint the inside of the box and lid with shellac.

6. Mix the gesso powder. Form the aluminum foil cone which is used to apply the gesso paste to the box.

7. Squeeze the gesso paste over the graphite lines on the lid. Work slowly so the gesso will form a ⅛-inch wide line, a little over ¹⁄₁₆ inch high. Outline the picture with gesso. When the lid is completely dry, add the gesso design to the front of the box. Let dry. Then add the designs to the sides and back of the box, letting each side dry before moving to the next area. Each side should face you as you work.

8. When all surfaces are thoroughly dry, cover wood and gesso with shellac. *Do not* add another coat of shellac to the picture—the one coat is enough.

9. Paint the outside surface of the box lid and gesso decoration with the metallic paint, using the ¾-inch flat brush. Use the #2 round brush to cover the gesso frame around the picture. Do not get any paint on the picture.

10. When the top of the lid is dry, paint the sides with metallic paint. When these are dry, paint the inside of the box with metallic paint, and let dry.

Variations: If you do not have any shellac, you can use two to three coats of metallic enamel.

If your box is a different size, make a freehand drawing of the design to the exact size of the box, and transfer to the lid with graphite paper.

GERMAN "GINGERBREAD" HOUSE

Gingerbread houses, in the Bavarian mountain style of southern Germany, are made from sheets of gingerbread cookie dough, and decorated with colored sugar icing.

However, the design in this book is made from balsa wood and decorated with colored gesso as a permanent "gingerbread house." This is a fairy-tale house that can be used Christmas after Christmas as a decoration for the holiday season.

Materials and Tools
2 balsa wood boards—6 x 36 x ¼ inches
2 square balsa wood dowels—36 x ½ x ½ inches
1 square balsa wood dowel—36 x ¼ x ¼ inches
1 triangular balsa wood dowel—36 x ½ inches
white lightweight cardboard or bristol board—
    2 x 5¼ inches
wood glue
medium sandpaper
string—3- to 4-yard length
wood stain—brown
small piece of cloth
gesso powder
tools for preparing and applying gesso
white shellac, or acrylic polymer gloss medium
acrylic paints—blue, red, white, and brown
newspapers
pencil
ruler
scissors
jeweler's saw or craft saw
craft knife
wood file
flat watercolor brush—¾ inch wide
round nylon brush—#3
paper clips

Directions

1. On the balsa wood boards, using ruler and pencil, measure out the separate pieces of the house. Follow the diagram for measurements and layout. Cut out the pieces with the saw. File the rough edges, and sandpaper the edges and flat surfaces. See pages 129-131 for information on working with wood.

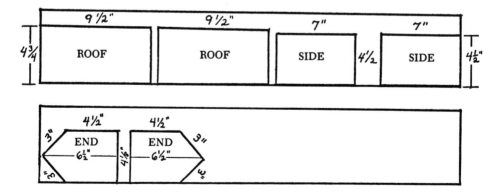

Layout of Pattern on Wood

2. Measure and cut the dowels into the following lengths:
½-inch square dowels: four 7-inch pieces, four 3½-inch pieces, two 2⅝-inch pieces;
¼-inch square dowel: four 2⅝-inch pieces, one 6½-inch piece;
½-inch triangular dowel: two 6½-inch pieces, two 1¼-inch pieces.
Smooth cut edges with file and sandpaper.

3. Glue the longer ½-inch square dowels to the inside bottom and top of the side pieces of the house, and the 3½-inch ones to the sides. Glue the 2⅝-inch lengths to the bottoms of the peaked end pieces. Then glue the 2⅝-inch pieces of ¼-inch dowels to the peaks of the end pieces, cutting off a small triangle from the bottom of each dowel to form a horizontal line. See diagram for placement of all dowels. Put the four pieces close together on a flat surface, dowel sides up, and place heavy books on top until the glue has hardened.

4. Glue the long sides and the narrow ends of the house together. Wrap string tightly around the house to hold the four sides together until the glue is hard.

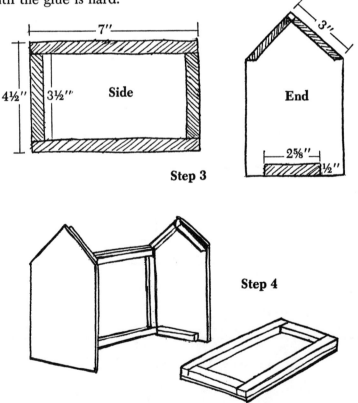

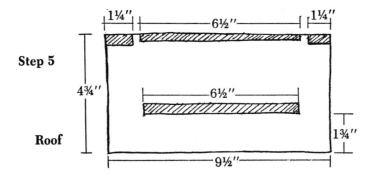

Step 5

Roof

5. Meanwhile, glue the two 6½-inch triangular dowels to the underside of the roof board, 1¾ inches above the lower edge of the roof, centering them on the 9½-inch length. Next, glue the 6½-inch piece of ¼-inch square dowel to the upper edge of one of the roof pieces, centering it on the 9½-inch length. Glue the two 1¼-inch triangular dowels at the ends of the same roof edge. See diagram for placement of all dowels. Place books on top of board and dowels until the glue is dry.

6. Stain the inside and outside of the roof sections with the brown stain. Dip the small piece of cloth into the stain; then rub it lightly into the wood. Remove string from the house when glue is dry, and stain the outside of the house with the brown stain.

7. Glue each of the two roof pieces to the sides and ends of the house. Let dry.

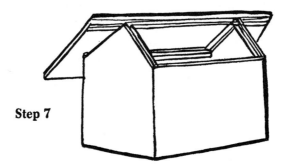

Step 7

8. Shellac the house and roof, using the ¾-inch flat watercolor brush, and let dry.

9. Use the grid method to enlarge the chimney diagram on the

Chimney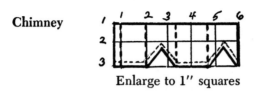

Enlarge to 1″ squares

lightweight cardboard, measuring it out with ruler and pencil. Cut it out with craft knife and ruler. Score the four long lines on the outside of the chimney with knife and ruler. Turn over and score the narrow margin lines. Fold the cardboard into the chimney shape, and put glue along the flap to hold the chimney together. Hold with a couple of paper clips until glue dries. Fold the bottom edge outward, and glue the chimney to the roof with these edges.

10. With the brown acrylic paint and the #3 round nylon brush, draw in the stone design on the chimney. Color the flaps brown to match the roof.

11. Mix the gesso and use an aluminum foil cone to apply the decorations to the house and roof. Follow drawing for placement of decorations. When the gesso is hard and dry, paint with acrylic colors, using the #3 round nylon brush. Mix the blue and red paints with white to make lighter shades. Colors are as follows: roof scallops—pink; edging of roof and hanging icicles—white; window shutters—medium blue with light blue edgings; heart decorations—red; window bars—light blue; door—deep pink with blue edge; decoration over door and side window—pink; edging around round window—light blue; edging at bottom of house—white. White icicles can be added to shutters and window frames. When paint is dry, cover the paint, gesso, and wood with a coat of shellac or acrylic polymer gloss medium, using the ¾-inch flat brush, and let dry.

Variations: All measurements can be doubled to make a larger house; the directions remain the same.

Metal Folk Arts

Techniques of Working with Metal

Working with metal is a little like working with paper, but it's not quite as easy. If the metal is thin and soft like aluminum, you can use special scissors called *jeweler's snips* to cut out a design. For harder metal, a *jeweler's saw* (also used for wood projects) is an easy tool to use. Cutting metal with it is a new skill to learn. It is easier to use a saw than snips, as cutting metal with snips needs strong hands.

Transferring a design

After you have made the final drawing of a design on a piece of typewriter paper, transfer it to the metal. First place a piece of carbon paper, shiny side down, on the metal. Lay the drawing on top of the carbon paper. Carbon paper and drawing paper should be only a little larger than the design. Hold both in place on the metal with pieces of masking tape. With a sharp-pointed pencil, draw over all the lines, pressing down heavily on the point. Before taking the drawing paper and carbon paper away, lift one corner of the carbon paper and peek under to see if all lines have been transferred. Redraw any that have been missed. Remove drawing and carbon paper.

Next, draw over all the lines on the metal with a *metal scriber*, as the carbon lines will rub off while you are sawing the metal. Wash off the carbon lines with rubbing alcohol or hot water and detergent.

A *metal scriber* is a tool that looks like a metal pencil. Instead of lead, it has a sharp point of metal which is used to make a thin line on

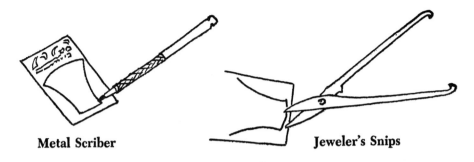

Metal Scriber   **Jeweler's Snips**

metal. The outline of the design will never be lost while you are working on a project.

Cutting with jeweler's snips

At craft or art stores, you can buy small, metal-cutting scissors called snips. They will cut through soft metal, such as tin or aluminum. Always cut just outside the scribed line around the design. After the piece has been cut from the metal, smooth all the cut edges with a *metal file*, right back to the scribed line. If any edges have curled while being cut with the snips, put a block of smooth wood over the whole piece of cutout metal. Tap all over the top of the wood block with a hammer. This will flatten the curled edges.

Cutting with a jeweler's saw

The metal frame is a C shape, with an oblong wooden handle attached to the bottom of the C. Thin saw blades of different sizes from 4/0 (finest) to 4 (coarsest) are held in the frame by wing nuts at top and bottom. The blades are sold in bundles of one dozen each. Sizes 2/0 or 1 are best for the projects in this book, both metal and wood.

You will also need a *bench pin*, which is a small board 7 x 2 ⅝ x ⅜ inches with a 2¾-inch long keyhole-shaped opening at the front. This is held to a table edge with a special C-clamp. Metal to be cut is put on top of the bench pin when sawing with the jeweler's saw.

Put a blade into the frame, teeth facing away from the frame and pointing down toward the handle. Loosen the top wing nut. Put the top of the blade between the two pieces of metal, and tighten the nut. Holding the handle in one hand, push the top of the frame against a solid vertical surface, such as a table edge. Now, loosen the bottom wing nut a bit, and put the bottom of the saw blade between the two pieces of metal. Tighten the wing nut, and take the saw away from the vertical surface. The blade is stretched tightly between the two wing nuts when the frame returns to its original shape.

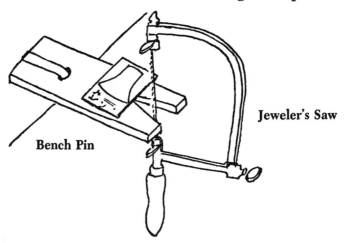

Jeweler's Saw

Bench Pin

Put the piece of metal, with the design marked by the scriber, on the bench pin. The line to be cut is always over the keyhole opening in the bench pin. Make a small notch in the edge of the metal with a file. Hold the saw frame upright, your hand grasping the handle at the bottom. Place the blade lightly in the notch at the edge of the metal and draw the blade downward, so the teeth just bite into the metal. Keep the blade very straight up-and-down. After cutting into the metal on the down stroke, pull the blade toward you a little so that it is not in contact with the metal for the return trip upward. Repeat the down-and-up movements until you have cut a line to the edge of the scribed design.

Then, very slowly, turn the metal with the fingertips of the other hand resting on the flat surface of the metal. At the same time make tiny down-and-up cutting movements of the saw blade. In this way you'll turn the corner and the scribed edge of the design will be facing away from you. Cut just outside the scribed line until you come to the next corner, then repeat the slow turn. If the design is a circle, just follow the circle, turning the metal slowly with the fingertips.

In other words, you are always sawing a piece of metal in a straight line away from you, as you saw over the keyhole opening in the bench pin. You turn the metal, rather than turning the saw, to follow the outline of the design.

You will break several blades in the process—everyone does, even experienced craftspeople. Just shorten the space between the wing nuts and insert the smaller piece of blade, or put in a new blade.

File all the edges smooth. Rub the surface of the metal with a fine piece of *crocus cloth* until it shines.

Filing metal

The thin files for metal work are smaller than the large wood files. They are 6 inches long and about ¼ inch wide, and are made in several shapes—flat, triangular, and half round. A flat, pointed file is the best all-around one for the projects in this book. Use the file to remove rough edges after cutting the metal design with either snips or saw. After all the edges are smooth, hold the file at a 45° angle; on the right side of the metal, file all around the edge from the top out to the bottom edge. This narrow, slanting edge makes the metal look thicker.

Filing Metal

Using crocus cloth

This is a very fine type of sandpaper, used in metalwork. It will remove all tiny scratches as you rub it across the metal surface. As you rub, the metal will be brightly polished.

FINNISH PENDANT

The original of this pendant is in the museum in Helsinski, Finland. It was made of silver in 1100 A.D. by a craftsperson of one of the tribes living in the north of Finland. These pieces are very rare, and the designs are no longer made, but Finnish craftspeople have continued to work with metal.

The metal used in this project is aluminum, which is much easier to cut and polish and is not as expensive as silver.

Materials and Tools
1 sheet of typewriter paper
1 sheet of carbon paper
1 piece of sheet aluminum—3 x 5 inches
2-tube epoxy cement
1 silver-colored jump ring
black cord—30-inch length
tools for working metal
pencil
ruler
toothpicks
aluminum foil—4 x 4 inches
small nail
hammer
2 pairs of pliers

Directions
1. Copy the pattern on the typewriter paper, using the grid method. Transfer it to the piece of sheet aluminum with the carbon paper.
2. Go over the carbon line on the metal with the metal scriber, including the pattern top and bottom and the outlines of the extra pieces of metal.

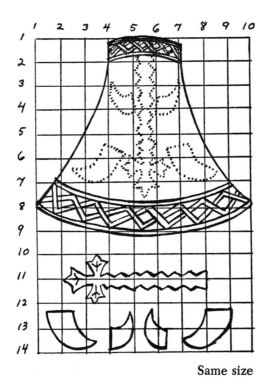

Same size

3. Cut around the scribed line of the pendant shape with either metal snips or jeweler's saw. Smooth the cut edges with a metal file, and polish the flat surface with crocus cloth. Also cut out the separate pieces; file and polish them.

4. With the scriber, deepen the lines of the border patterns. Use a ruler as a straight edge so the lines will be straight and sharp.

5. Wash the metal with detergent to remove carbon lines if any are left after polishing. Detergent will also remove grease left by your fingers, so the epoxy cement will hold on the surface.

6. Cement the separate pieces of metal to the surface of the pendant as shown by the scribed lines. Follow manufacturer's directions on the tubes of epoxy cement. Use toothpicks and aluminum foil for the mixing.

7. When the pieces of metal are in place, put a heavy weight carefully on top of the pendant. Let it stay in place for several hours.

When you remove the weight, check the pendant carefully to be sure that all pieces are held firmly in place. If not, re-cement.

8. Make a hole at the top of the pendant with a small nail. Drive the nail in from *front to back*, using a hammer. File the rough edges on the back until they are smooth.

9. Open the jump ring. Use pliers to move the metal apart in opposite directions at the join of the ring. Slip the jump ring through the hole in the pendant. Close the jump ring with the pliers. Run the cord through the ring, and tie in a bow at the back of your neck. The pendant should hang about three inches below the front edge of your collar bone.

MEXICAN LANTERN

All over Mexico, craftspeople have used tin cans to make candle holders of many types, mirror frames, crowns to wear in processions, and many other decorative objects. Candle holders are set on tables or hung from the ceiling alone or in groups that hang at different levels. The candlelight shining through the holes casts patterns on the walls and ceiling—the more candle holders, the more patterns.

Enlarge to 1″ squares

Materials and Tools
empty, smooth-sided tin can—
   7 inches high, 4¼ inches in diameter
newspapers
1 sheet of typewriter paper
1 sheet of carbon paper
masking tape
short, thick votive candle
pencil
ruler
scissors
felt-tipped black marking pen
thin nail
hammer

Directions
1. Clean the inside of the can and remove paper label and glue. Leave the bottom of the can in place.
2. Cut several sections of newspaper. Pile strips on top of each other, then roll up very tightly. The tight roll should be the same diameter as the can. Hold the shape by wrapping masking tape around the roll in four places. Put roll inside the can.
3. Enlarge the pattern by the grid method on the typewriter paper. Cut out pattern along the outside edges.
4. Cut a strip of carbon paper the same height as the can, and long enough to wrap around the can, carbon side against the tin. Add an extra strip of carbon paper to fill out the 13½-inch length. Hold both pieces in place with small pieces of masking tape. Place the paper pattern on top of the carbon paper, left-hand edge against the seamline of the can, and hold in place with small pieces of masking tape.
5. Transfer the pattern to the surface of the can, using a sharp pencil to trace over the lines. Repeat pattern two more times around the can.
6. Remove carbon paper. Go over the carbon paper marks with the felt-tipped pen, making round dots.

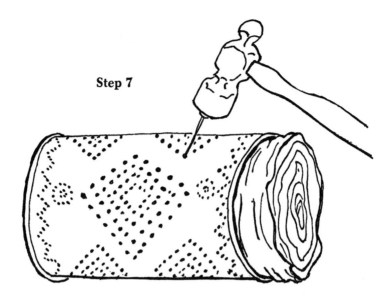

Step 7

7. Then, with the nail and hammer, punch holes in the can at every spot where there is a pen mark.

8. When all the holes have been punched in the can, remove the newspaper roll.

9. Heat the bottom of the can by placing it over the pilot light area of the stove. Remove from heat when bottom is hot. Place candle inside, in the center of the bottom. The heat will melt a little of the wax on the bottom of the candle. When the bottom has cooled, the candle will be held firmly in place.

10. Light the candle and watch the flickering pattern of light against the wall or ceiling.

Paper Folk Arts
❖ ❖ ❖

Techniques of Working with Paper
Both the supplies and tools for making projects with paper are very simple. In fact, the tools are in every home—ruler, pencil, eraser, and scissors, both small and large. Other tools are easily bought in art and craft stores and can be used for other projects. A ¾-inch flat watercolor or nylon brush for smoothing on the glue is also used for other crafts. A sharp-pointed craft knife is needed to cut cardboard and illustration board. You will use this knife also for stencil and wood crafts.

You will be using several types of paper and cardboard, and they are listed in each project. Thin paper will be needed for the Japanese kite. Lightweight white cardboard or bristol board is best for the Indian walking elephant and the stenciled Swedish bookends. Plain gray cardboard, colored construction paper, watercolor paper, contact paper, and illustration board are also used in several of the projects in this book.

Here are general instructions for working with paper or cardboard.

Drawing on paper

Always measure the final drawing with a ruler. Draw light pencil lines that can be easily erased if necessary. When erasing a line on paper, spread thumb and forefinger apart, pressing down on the paper at the area to be erased. Then erase pencil lines or smudges between the two fingers. The pressure of your fingers will keep the paper from creasing if the eraser catches it. Use a pink rubber eraser for all pencil lines, and an artgum kneadable eraser for graphite lines.

Cutting paper

Scissors are the best tool for cutting thin paper. When using a craft knife to cut heavy paper or cardboard, always brace the knife against the edge of a ruler; this way the cut will be straight, and you can repeat it in the same place if the first cut does not go through the cardboard or paper.

Gluing paper

Thin out white household glue with a little water, so it can be brushed on with a soft ¾-inch flat watercolor brush. Put the glue on the paper in a thin coat. It is best to put glue on both facing pieces of cardboard for a stronger bond, as cardboard will absorb the glue.

ENGLISH VICTORIAN PRESSED FLOWERS

In the early 1800's, English ladies began pressing flowers and plants between the pages of large books. This dried material was then arranged on a sheet of paper. When covered with glass and a frame, the picture was hung on a wall. Sometimes the designs were used on glass-covered tea trays. The craft spread to Europe and to America. Often the flowers had special meaning; they might be cut from a friend's garden, saved from a wedding bouquet, gathered during a trip to a foreign country, or kept as a memory of some other happy time.

Materials and Tools
dried flowers, grasses, and small tips of ferns
typewriter paper
heavy book
watercolor paper or any heavy paper
thin cardboard (optional)
white household glue
face tissues
wax paper
clear plastic wrap
cellophane tape
pencil
ruler
scissors
jar top or other small container
round watercolor brush—#2
satin ribbon—⅜ inch wide by 6 inches long
cord for hanging picture—8-inch length

Directions
1. You will have to make preparations one or two weeks ahead for this project. Pick any flowers with stems, even small rosebuds, some leaves, grasses, and ferns that will fit the size paper to be used.
2. Arrange a flower with its stem and leaves on a sheet of typewriter paper. Cover with a second sheet of paper. Add a third sheet of paper, arrange another flower, or a spray of grass with a seed head, or a short tip of a fern leaf on it. Cover with a fourth sheet of paper. Keep adding to the pile until you have used ten or twelve flowers, grasses, and ferns. Each plant part should have its own bottom and top sheet of paper, so that each plant part can be arranged without disturbing the pressing below.
3. Put a heavy book over the last sheet of paper. Let the pile stand for a week without moving it. At the end of a week, lift up the book and peek into the pile. If the plants are not dry enough, put the book back on top of the pile. Check again in a few days.

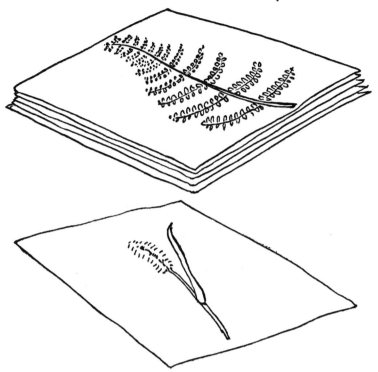

4. When plants are dry, measure and cut out with the scissors the size sheet of paper you will need for the final card or picture.

For a picture to hang on the wall: a single sheet of heavy paper, 7 x 10 inches, glued to a piece of thin cardboard the same size. For a card to send to a friend: a single sheet of heavy paper, 5½ x 8½ inches, folded in half along the 8½-inch length. This will make a double card, 5½ inches high and 4¼ inches wide.

5. Spread the sheets of dried plants on a flat surface. Pick out the flowers, grasses, and ferns that will make the best picture. Put them in the center of the paper to make a pleasing design. Try to bring all the stems together like a bouquet. Handle the plant material carefully, as it will be brittle.

6. The next step is to glue the material to the paper. Put a teaspoon of white glue in a jar top or any other small container. Add a little water to the glue, and mix together. The mixture should be thin enough to brush on easily.

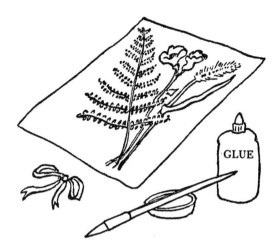

7. Lift up each piece of plant material and, with the brush dipped in the glue, add glue to the bottom of the flower, leaves, and stem. Press down lightly in the same position on the paper. Dab gently with a crumpled piece of face tissue. Repeat this process until all the plant material is in place.

8. Tie the ribbon into a small bow. Add glue to the back of the bow and press it in place over the stems, as if it were holding the material together.

9. Place a sheet of wax paper over the whole picture and put a heavy book on top until the glue is dry. When dry, check for any loose pieces, and re-glue them.

10. When everything is dry, cut a piece of clear plastic wrap, ½ inch larger on all sides than the card or picture. Use this to cover the surface of the card or picture, protecting the plant material. Turn over the extra ½ inch of clear plastic to the back of the paper. Hold in place with cellophane tape.

11. Write a message inside the card. If the design is a picture, tape a short length of cord to the back, 2 inches down from the top edge, and 1 inch in from each edge. Hang on the wall.

FRENCH DECOUPAGE WASTEBASKET

Decoupage is a French word meaning the art of cutting out. It is used to describe the cutting out of printed paper designs to decorate various objects. This craft began in the eighteenth century at the French court where furniture with painted designs became popular. Court ladies, who were not artists, cut out designs of flowers, birds and scenes from printed papers. They pasted the cutouts on trays, boxes, or small pieces of wood furniture. Wood and paper were then covered with varnish. Some pieces are still preserved in museums. In this project a metal wastebasket is the base for the cutout design.

Materials and Tools
solid-color Contact paper—1 yard
metal wastepaper basket
colored pictures cut from a magazine,
    wallpaper sample, or prints
white household glue
acrylic polymer gloss medium, or polyurethane varnish
pencil
ruler
scissors
flat watercolor brush—¾ inch wide
flat nylon brush—¾ inch wide
small container for mixing glue

Directions

1. On the back side, measure the Contact paper to fit the outside of the wastepaper basket. Cut the Contact paper to size with the scissors. Follow the manufacturer's directions for applying the paper to the surface of the metal wastepaper basket.

2. Cut out a picture to be glued on the front of the wastepaper basket. The picture can be in color or black-and-white. Here are several suggestions:

a square, round, oval, or rectangular picture, cut out along the edges;

part of a picture, cut out along the edge of the object—a flower, a building, an animal, or a person;

several objects cut from different pictures, arranged to make a new design;

several pictures placed on different areas of the wastepaper basket, so that there are pictures on all sides.

3. Mix glue with a little water in the small container, and use the ¾-inch watercolor brush to apply glue to the pictures. Place them carefully on the wastepaper basket.

4. When the glue is dry, cover picture and Contact paper with acrylic polymer gloss medium or polyurethane varnish, using the ¾-inch nylon brush.

Variations: Use this process to cover plastic tissue boxes, trays, metal cookie containers, kitchen canisters, or an empty tea tin to hold tea bags for the dinner table.

INDIAN WALKING ELEPHANT

Ancient Indian wall and miniature paintings show elephants with decorated fabric saddles and headpieces. Their necks are hung with jeweled leather collars, and even their ivory tusks are brightly painted. These were elephants who walked in religious or state processions, or carried maharajas on their backs. This walking elephant is copied from one of those early paintings.

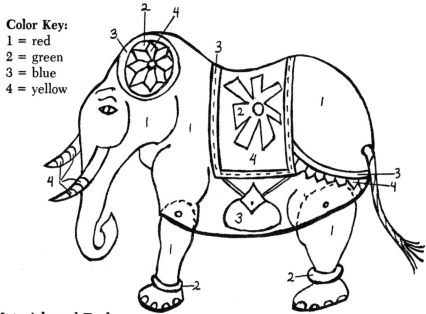

Color Key:
1 = red
2 = green
3 = blue
4 = yellow

Materials and Tools
1 sheet of typewriter paper
1 sheet of graphite paper
lightweight illustration board or white cardboard—
    6½ x 8½ inches
acrylic paints—black, dark red, bright green, and
    lemon yellow
stiff wire or coat hanger wire—8½-inch length
string—8-inch length
adhesive tape—¾ inch wide
pencil
ruler
scissors
flat nylon brush—¾ inch wide
round nylon brush—#3
felt-tipped black waterproof pen
craft knife
small thin nail
wire cutter
pliers

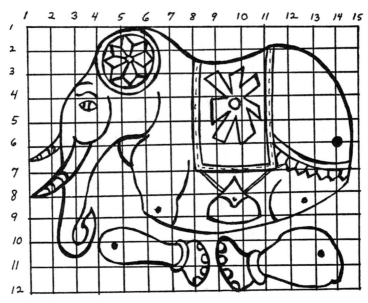

Enlarge to ½" squares

Directions

1. Enlarge the elephant pattern on the typewriter paper by the grid method. With graphite paper, transfer the enlarged drawing to the illustration board or white cardboard.

2. Thin out the black acrylic paint and cover the body and legs with a thin, light gray wash. Let dry.

3. Outline the elephant's body and legs with the black felt-tipped pen. Follow the graphite paper transfer lines. Also outline all the decorations on the body of the elephant. Let dry.

4. With either the scissors or the craft knife, cut along the outside edge of the black body and legs outline.

5. Add colored decorations with acrylic paints and #3 brush to the saddle, head, body, and tusks. Follow the colors on the printed pattern, or choose your own colors.

6. When the paint is dry, punch two holes with the nail at the bottom edge of the elephant's body as shown on the pattern. Also punch a hole at the top of each leg.

7. With the scissors, cut two 2-inch pieces of string. Tie a knot at one end of each piece. Pull the unknotted end of one piece, front to back, through one hole at the bottom edge of the elephant's body. Then push the string, front to back, through the top hole in one leg. Pull the string all the way through until the knot is against the elephant's body. The leg should be close to the body, but able to move freely. Tie a knot against the back of the leg, and with the scissors cut off the extra string. Repeat with the other leg and piece of string.

8. To add the elephant's tail, punch a hole with the nail at the back of the body, as shown on the pattern. Tie a knot at one end of the rest of the string. Pull string through the hole, front to back. Tie a second knot close to the body, to hold the string in place. Fray the other end of the string. Trim the string so that the free end is about ½ inch shorter than the legs.

9. Stick a 2-inch long piece of adhesive tape across the back surface of the elephant. Follow the drawing for placement of the tape. Leave a vertical loop in the center, a little broader than the thickness of the wire.

10. Cut a piece of coat hanger wire with wire cutters and then bend it with pliers to match the drawing.

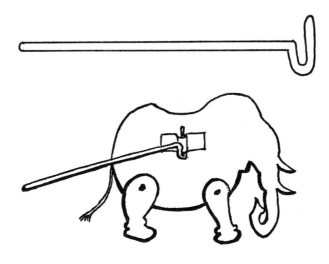

11. To make the elephant walk, insert the hook end of the wire into the adhesive loop, from the bottom to the top (see drawing). Hold the other end of the wire and move the elephant forward, feet just touching the ground.

ITALIAN "STAINED GLASS" WINDOW

Glass making in Europe began in Venice, brought there from the Middle East. The craft spread across north Italy, and stained glass windows were put in place in the cathedral at Assisi as early as the thirteenth century. At that time, flat glass could only be made in small pieces, so these colored sections of glass had to be held together by strips of lead (the softest metal) to form a large window. The lead strips also served to outline the design. In cathedrals and castles, stained glass windows "told" stories to those who could not read.

Stained glass projects need a lot of special tools, and a great deal of skill in cutting glass, bending metal, and soldering it in place. Instead, this project is the first step in designing a window. It is the craftsperson's way of making a scale model, using paper to plan the sizes of the pieces of glass and the placement of the colors and the lead strips. Many "thumbnail" sketches of this type can be easily made until the final design pleases the craftsperson. This project also shows you part of the town of Assisi in Italy.

Materials and Tools

2 sheets of typewriter paper
1 sheet of black construction
    paper—8½ x 11-inches
1 sheet of graphite paper
white household glue
watercolor paints—blue, brown,
    green, red, yellow, and black
double-sided tape
1-inch wide black masking tape (optional)

pencil
ruler
small pointed scissors
round watercolor brushes—
    #3 and #8
face tissues

Enlarge to ½″ squares

Directions

1. Enlarge the picture of an Italian hill town on a sheet of typewriter paper by the grid method. Transfer the drawing to the right side of the black construction paper, using graphite paper.

2. Hold the black construction paper at a slight angle so the light will catch the graphite lines. Cut out the design with scissors. When you are finished, you will have a connecting web of black paper lines. The paper lines give the effect of the strips of lead separating pieces of colored glass in a stained glass window.

3. Put the black cutout over the second sheet of typewriter paper. With the pencil, lightly trace around the edges of all the openings in the black paper cutout. Remove the black paper and lay it aside.

4. Now paint in the colors, following the notes on the drawing. Carry the colors over the pencil lines, to just outside them. Use as little water as possible so the paper will not wrinkle. Apply paint in the small areas with the #3 brush, and use the #8 brush for the large areas. Mix colors in several tones to add interest to the picture.

Color Key:
1 = light blue
2 = green
3 = dark yellow
4 = light rust red
5 = gray
6 = white

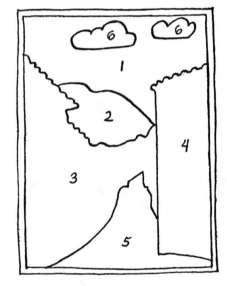

5. When the colors are dry, put the sheet to one side. Turn the black cutout sheet to the wrong side. Squeeze white glue into a small dish and add a little water to thin the glue. Using a #3 brush, lightly paint over the black lines with the thinned-out glue. Stay inside all the edges, so the glue will not ooze out onto the colored sheet when the black cutout is placed on top.

6. Quickly put the black sheet of paper, glue side down, over the colored sheet of paper. Dab the black lines with a crumpled face tissue, pressing them into place. Blot any glue with the tissue if it does ooze out from the edges.

7. Put a large book—a telephone book is fine—over the two sheets of paper until the glue is dry.

8. Place the picture on the inside of a window glass, black lines facing toward the room. Hold it in place with double-sided sticky tape. If your home has small-paned windows, make the design just the size of one of the window sections. If you like, bind the edge of the picture with black masking tape before attaching it to the window glass.

Variation: You can lay a sheet of tracing paper over a picture in a magazine, and make your own design.

JAPANESE BUTTERFLY KITE

The Japanese have always made and flown kites. These are of colored or painted paper supported by thin strips of bamboo or

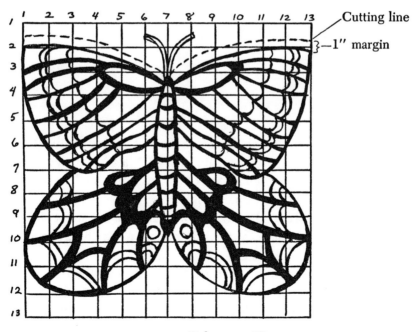

Enlarge to 2″ squares

lightweight wood. Some are fighting kites or special festival kites, and others are just-flying-for-fun kites. They are made in many shapes and sizes, and the butterfly kite is one of the favorites.

Materials and Tools
1 sheet of white paper—24 x 24 inches
2 sheets of graphite paper—18 x 24 inches
masking tape—1 inch wide
1 sheet of rice paper or thin vellum paper—
   24 x 36 inches
wide felt-tipped black waterproof pen
acrylic paints—red, orange, and yellow
2 balsa wood dowels—12½ x ¼ x ¹⁄₁₆ inches
1 balsa wood dowel—14½ x ¼ x ¹⁄₁₆ inches
2 balsa wood dowels—22 x ¹⁄₁₆ x ¹⁄₁₆ inches
nylon or cord fishing line
white glue
ruler
pencil
scissors
flat nylon brush—¾ inch wide
craft saw or knife
small plastic container for mixing paints

Directions
1. Soak the two 22-inch dowels in water to cover for two hours to make it easier to bend them into a curve. Make a 3-inch split in one end of the 14½-inch dowel. Soak this dowel too, so that each side of the split can be bent into an angle.
2. Measure and cut off a 7 x 24-inch piece from one sheet of graphite paper. Tape this piece to the other sheet along the 24-inch edge. You will then have a piece 24 x 24 inches.
3. Enlarge the butterfly pattern by the grid method on the plain sheet of white paper. Measure and cut the rice paper with the scissors to a 24 x 24-inch sheet. Using the graphite paper, transfer

the butterfly design to the rice paper. Remove the graphite paper and the white paper pattern.

4. Draw over all the graphite lines on the rice paper with the felt-tipped pen. Let pen lines dry.

5. Color the areas between the lines with thinned-out acrylic paints. Follow the color notes on the drawing. Let paint dry.

Color Key:
1 = orange
2 = red
3 = yellow

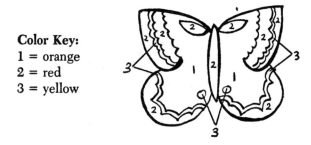

6. While the paint is drying, turn over the white paper butterfly pattern. Enlarge, by the grid method, the curved shapes of the dowels for the back of the butterfly kite. Also mark the placement of the other three dowels and the nylon cord. Then, with graphite paper, transfer the lines to the back of the painted butterfly.

7. Take the two 22-inch dowels out of the water and dry them. Gently curve the wood, starting in the middle of the dowel, stroking it between thumb and forefinger of each hand. Place them over the paper pattern and finish curving the dowels, following the pencil lines. Hold them in place with short pieces of masking tape until they are completely dry. When dry, they will stay in their curved shapes.

Next, remove the 14½-inch dowel from the water and dry it. Curve and angle the two sides of the 3-inch split, following the pattern. Hold in place with small pieces of masking tape until dry.

8. Cut along the outside margin of the painted butterfly, using the scissors. Leave a 1-inch margin of paper along the top edge of the butterfly's wings.

Back View

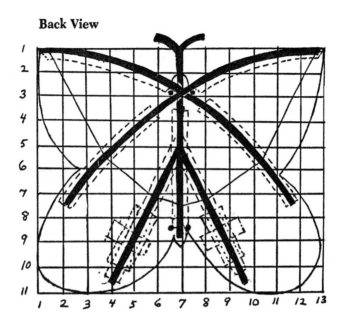

Steps 9-10

9. *Refer to the drawing for all the steps described in 9 and 10.* Tie the center of a 40-inch length of nylon line to the bottom of the 14½-inch dowel, 1 inch above the end. Glue this center dowel in position. Hold in place with masking tape covering the full length of the dowel. Place the two 12½-inch dowels in position, wrapping the nylon line once around each dowel before gluing the dowels in place. Cover dowels with masking tape. Finally, put the two 22-inch curved dowels in position, looping the nylon line around the ends, about 5 inches above the lower ends. You might want to hold the lower ends in place with a small piece of masking tape. Then bring each end of the line straight up on each side to the top of the curved dowels, and tie to the outer ends of each dowel, 1 inch in from the ends. Glue the dowels in position. Turn the top 1-inch margin of paper over the dowels and glue in position. Cover dowels and paper turn-over with masking tape.

10. From the leftover rice paper, cut two 20-inch long strips, 1 inch wide. Fold each one in half, then in half again so that you have two pieces, 5 inches long and 1 inch wide. Glue the bottom of the folded strip over the bottom of the lefthand dowel; repeat with the other folded strip on the righthand dowel. Hold each one in place with a horizontal piece of masking tape.

11. Cut a 42-inch length of nylon line. Wrap one end around the place where the curved dowels cross each other; then make two small holes in the paper at this place, one on each side of the center dowel. Bring the short piece of the line through one hole and the long piece through the other hole. Tie together on the front of the kite. Bring the long end of the line down the front of the kite. Make

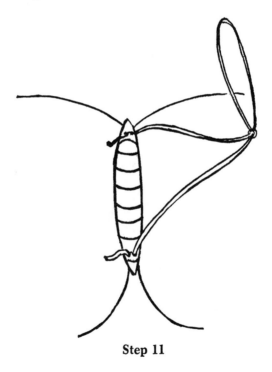

Step 11

two more holes at the bottom of the center dowel; put the end of the line through one hole, across the dowel, and up through the other hole. Tie together at the front as above. Then hold the line straight out from the front of the kite; make a knot about 10 inches down to form a long loop. The full length of the kite string will be attached to the center of this loop (see drawing).

12. Wait for a clear, windy day to launch your kite. You can also hang the butterfly from the ceiling or the wall as a room decoration.

THAI FESTIVAL OF LIGHTS CANDLE

In Thailand and other South Asian areas, the Festival of Lights is an offering to the water gods at the end of the rainy season when the rice has been planted. Small boats (called *Kratong*) in the shape of lotus flowers, carrying candles, are set adrift on the rivers and canals. In the light of a full moon, they float on the dark waters, the small candle lights sparkling in the night. The boats are made from folded banana leaves wrapped around a disk cut from a banana stalk. Ours are made from aluminum foil, so they will not catch fire as they float in a wide bowl of water on a table.

Materials and Tools

sheet of aluminum foil—12 x 52½ inches
sheet of aluminum foil—2½ x 5 inches
1 aluminum foil cupcake pan—3⅝ inches in diameter
1 sheet of typewriter paper
narrow jar—5 inches tall, 2 inches in diameter (or less)
1 tube of acrylic latex contact cement
votive candle—1 inch high, 1½ inches in diameter
ruler
pencil
scissors
compass

Directions

1. You will need 24 aluminum foil petals for this project. Each petal is 4⅝ inches long and 1¾ inches wide, and is made from foil strips folded over three times so that each petal is made of three thicknesses of foil. For this you will need six strips of foil, 17½ inches long and 5¼ inches wide. Spread a thin layer of contact cement all over one side of each strip. Fold each strip over on itself lengthwise (adding cement to each exposed surface) so that each strip measures 1¾ inches wide, and 17½ inches long. Let cement dry.
2. Enlarge the petal pattern on the typewriter paper by the grid method. Cut out the pattern with the scissors along the pencil outline.

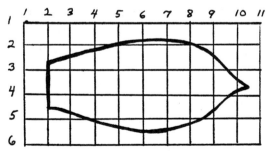

Enlarge to ½″ squares

3. Lay the pattern over the end of one strip of folded foil, and cut around the edges with the scissors through all three layers. Repeat until you have cut four 3-layered petals from the strip. Repeat with the other five strips so that you have 24 petals in all.

4. With the compass, mark two 2-inch circles on the small piece of aluminum foil. Cut out the two circles with the scissors, and set them aside.

5. Pull the flat edge of the aluminum foil cupcake pan into an upright position. Turn the pan over and place it on top of the jar.

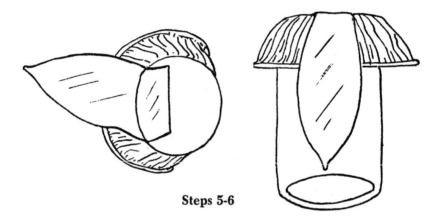

Steps 5-6

6. You will now add a row of six petals around the outside of the pan, slightly overlapping the petals. (Each petal has three layers.) The petals will meet in the center of the bottom of the pan, and curve up over the sides of the pan. Put them into position first, then glue them in place. Follow the manufacturer's directions on the tube of contact cement.

7. When the petals are dry, cover the bottom section with one of the 2-inch circles of aluminum foil. Glue in place and let dry before proceeding.

8. Now turn the pan over and place six petals inside around the sides of the pan and covering the bottom of the pan. The petal points should be placed between the points of the outside row of petals.

Cover the bottom and inside wall of the pan with glue, as well as the bottom of petals, and place in position; follow manufacturer's directions. When dry, add a second row of petals, points between the points of the first inside row. When dry, add a third row. These last two rows are glued only half way up the wall, to allow them to be curved forward a bit.

9. Cover bottom of the petals with the second circle of aluminum foil, glueing it into position. Let dry thoroughly.

10. When dry, curve the two inside rows of petals inward. With thumb and forefinger, press a slight lengthwise crease in each petal.

11. Melt the bottom of the candle briefly, and while it is still soft, press it into the inside of the petaled pan. Hold in place until the wax cools and hardens and holds the candle steady. Set the petaled candle holder in a wide dish of water so that it floats. Then light the candle. You can make several holders and float them in a large dish as a table centerpiece.

Papier-Mache Folk Arts
❖ ❖ ❖

Techniques of Working with Papier-Mache
Papier-mache is not only an easy craft, it is also a recycling one as it uses newspaper as the basic material.

First, tear or cut newspapers into strips, ½ inch wide and as long as the sheet of paper. Next mix a bowl of paste, the amount depending on the project you are making. If it is a large one, and you run out of paste, just make a second bowl full. Start with ½ cup of flour; then slowly add ¼ cup of water, stirring all the time so that the flour will not lump. When it is well mixed, add enough water to make a thin paste. Add 1 tablespoon of white glue or wood glue to the flour and water mixture, and stir until well mixed.

Pour the paste into a wide, shallow dish. Pull strips of paper through the paste and wrap them around a mold. Several layers of paper are crisscrossed over each other to build up a thickness of ⅛ to ¼ inches or more, all over the mold. After you have built up the right thickness of paper, let the object dry.

FRENCH FLEUR-DE-LIS BOWL

In France in the eighteenth century, small boxes and bowls made of papier-mache were very popular. These were easy to make, light in weight, and looked very much like the more expensive objects made of glass enamel on precious metal.

This project is a small bowl, painted dark blue and decorated with a gold fleur-de-lis pattern—the symbol of the French kings.

Materials and Tools
small pudding or mixing bowl—5 inches in diameter
   at the top, 3¼ inches high (2¾ inches up to the rim)
small can of white shellac
acrylic paint—cobalt blue
acrylic polymer gloss medium
small jar of metallic hobby enamel—gold or brass
flat nylon brush—¾ inch wide
round watercolor brush—#2
medium sandpaper
materials and tools for papier-mache

Directions
1. Prepare the newspapers and mix the paste for papier-mache (see page 110).
2. Turn the small mixing bowl upside down on the working surface, and cover it to just below the rim with a ¼-inch thick layer of paper and paste. Crisscross the strips in all directions.
3. Let the papier-mache dry until it is stiff enough to hold its shape. Do not let it dry too much, as it will shrink tightly against the mold, making removal difficult. Remove from the mold and place the papier-mache bowl upright to dry.
4. When bowl is completely dry, sandpaper it inside and out until all surfaces are smooth. Remove all traces of dust.
5. Turn the bowl upside down and cover the outside surface with two coats of shellac, applied with the ¾-inch flat nylon brush, to seal

the paper. Let dry between coats, sandpapering both coats when dry. Turn the bowl right side up, and repeat the shellacking and sandpapering on the inside surface of the bowl.

6. Turn the bowl upside down and paint the outside surface with two or three coats of cobalt blue acrylic paint; thin the paint with enough acrylic polymer gloss medium so that it can be easily applied with the ¾-inch nylon brush. Sandpaper all coats as they dry, except the last one. Then, turning the bowl right side up, repeat the painting and sandpapering on the inside surface of the bowl.

7. Decorate the top edge of the bowl with a ½-inch band of metallic enamel. Then paint gold fleur-de-lis over the surface of the bowl, inside and out. Use the #2 round watercolor brush for this purpose. See drawing for the pattern to follow for the decorations. Let paint dry. You can then cover the whole surface with acrylic polymer gloss medium, using the ¾-inch nylon brush, for a high-gloss finish.

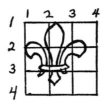

Reduce to ⅛" squares

MEXICAN PIGGY BANK

The craft of papier-mache was brought to Mexico in the late eighteenth to early nineteenth centuries by European settlers. It was an inexpensive and quick way of making objects that usually were made of fired clay. Tree designs, covered with tiny figures and holders for candles; mirror and picture frames; *pinata* figures stuffed with small candies; these are only a few of the decorative objects made by craftspeople. Here is a papier-mache pig, very much like a *pinata*, only smaller. It is painted with designs, Mexican style, with a slit in the top for coins.

Color Key:
1 = white
2 = bright blue
3 = cerise
4 = bright green

Materials and Tools
balloon—4 inches long
string—4-inch length
white household glue
1 sheet of typewriter paper
1 sheet of graphite paper
1 sheet of heavy drawing paper—8 x 11 inches
materials and tools for papier-mache
medium sandpaper
acrvlic paints—bright blue, cerise,
   bright green, and white
acrylic polymer gloss medium
pencil
ruler
scissors
craft knife (optional)
flat nylon brush—¾ inch wide
round nylon brushes—#3 and #8
2 water glasses

Directions

1. Blow up the balloon until it is 6 inches long. Tie with a piece of string, ¼ inch in from the blowing end. Hold tied end upright and fill the small opening with white glue. Brace the balloon in upright position until the glue dries. This will keep the air from leaking out of the balloon.

2. Draw the cone pattern for the legs on the typewriter paper, using the grid method. Transfer it to the drawing paper, using graphite paper. You will need four cones, so repeat pattern three more times. Cut out the cones with the scissors. Curl each paper cutout into a cone form. Glue down the seams with white household glue. Let dry.

3. Copy and transfer the pattern for the ears to the drawing paper. You will need two ears.

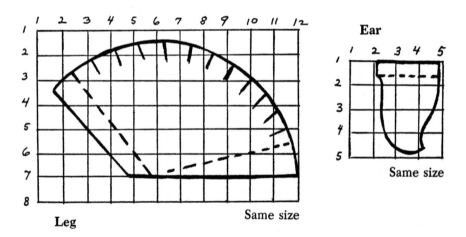

Leg   Same size

Ear   Same size

4. Mix the flour and water paste and prepare the newspaper strips (see page 110).

5. Cover the balloon with crisscrossed strips of newspaper dipped in the paste. After two layers of newspaper strips, put the four cones in place at the bottom of the balloon. These are the pig's legs. Fold back the top edge of each cone ⅜ inch, making cuts ¼ inch apart all around the edge. Cover the folded-back edge with paste and stick each cone to the newspaper body. See drawing for position.

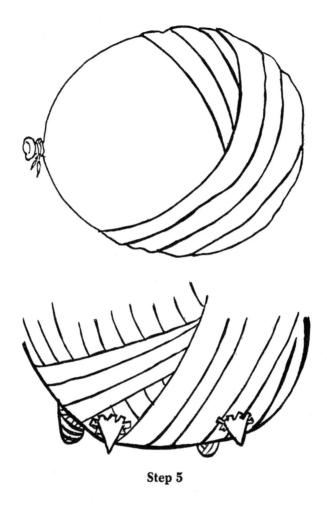

Step 5

6. Continue to cover the balloon and cones until the papier-mache is ¼ to ⅜ inch thick. Add narrow strips of newspaper around the tied-off end of the balloon, to form the pig's snout.

7. Dip the ears into the paste until the paper is covered on both sides. Hang the ears over a pencil balanced between two water glasses. When the ears are stiff, put them in place with the paste. Cover the folded-over flaps with strips of newspaper.

8. Let the papier-mache dry until it is hard. Then go over the newspaper surface with sandpaper to smooth out any bumpy places.

9. Paint the pig with two coats each of gloss medium and white acrylic paint, using the ¾-inch flat nylon brush; let dry between coats. Add the designs (see drawing on page 113) in cerise, blue, and green with the #3 and #8 round nylon brushes.

10. When all the paint is dry, cut a slot in the top of the pig. Use sharp-pointed scissors or a craft knife. Make it large enough so the coins will go in easily—and large enough so you can get them out! Touch up the edges with paint.

11. Finally, add a coat of clear acrylic polymer gloss medium with the ¾-inch flat nylon brush over the whole surface. Let dry.

P.S. The balloon stays inside the pig.

Stenciled Folk Arts

❖ ❖ ❖

Techniques of Working with Stencils

Stenciling is a way of exactly repeating a design; it may be used to make a border or an allover pattern, to decorate fabric or other material, or to make a number of similar greeting cards. A single stencil is cut for a complete design in one color. A design can be made in two or three colors, with a separate stencil cut for each one.

Cutting out a stencil

Stencil paper is a special type of paper which is sold in art and craft stores. The other materials and tools needed for making a stencil are:

sheets of white typewriter paper for the first drawing

a piece of cardboard at least 1 inch larger than the typewriter paper

masking tape

pencil

ruler

felt-tipped black marking pen

craft knife

Enlarge any of the stencil project designs in this book on a sheet of typewriter paper by the grid method. If you are making your own design, then make a drawing to the exact size of the final design. With a pencil, darken the sections to be cut out, so you will know what the colored design will look like. All openings must be separated by paper "lines" which are attached to each other.

For both of the above, trace over the pencil lines with the felt-tipped pen. Tape the drawing to the cardboard with the masking tape. Cut the stencil paper to a size a little larger than the drawing outlines. Place it over the design, taping the edges with masking tape.

Hold the knife like a pencil, bringing it toward you as you cut into the stencil paper, following the black outlines of the design beneath it. When all the areas are cut out, remove the stencil paper from the cardboard. Tape the stencil to whatever surface is to be decorated.

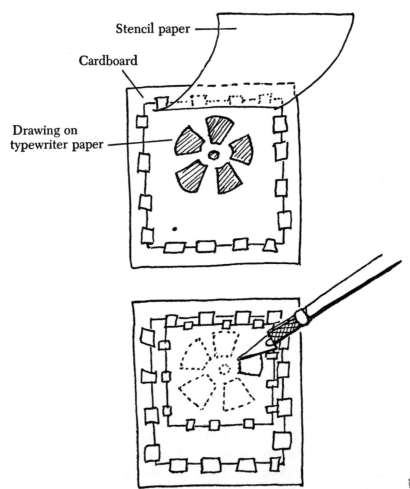

Stencil paper

Cardboard

Drawing on typewriter paper

Painting a stencil

To add color through the cutout stencil design, you will need a tube or tubes of acrylic paint and a stencil brush, which is a round, ¾-inch wide, flat-bottomed brush. Squeeze only a small ribbon of acrylic paint on a plastic coffee can top or a throwaway aluminum foil pie plate. With an up-and-down movement, touch the end of the brush to the paint; then lightly dab it on newspaper to get rid of excess paint and to spread the paint across the surface hairs of the brush. Dab the paint in the stencil design openings, holding the brush upright. When the design has been completed, remove the tape and lift the stencil paper straight up—quickly, so as not to smear the edges of the design. Let the paint dry without moving the decorated surface. Wash the brush in water and wipe dry with paper towels. When the paint is completely dry, go on to the next design, repeating the above processes.

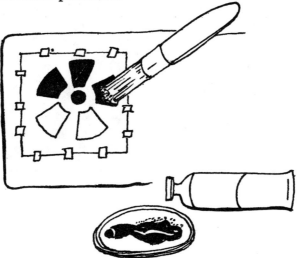

If you are stenciling a design that has two or more colors, go straight through with one color on the number of pieces you have to make. Wash up brushes and paint holder, and let the paint dry. Then put the second stencil in place; squeeze out the second color; and follow directions in the last paragraph. Follow this procedure for each additional color. Or you can add separate colors to different sections of one stencil.

CARIBBEAN SCARF

All through the Caribbean islands, scarves are worn to protect the head from sun or sudden showers. On some islands, the various ways the scarves are tied have special meanings; they may indicate that the wearer is unmarried, married, or widowed. Colors and designs are suggested by the local plants and flowers. Coconut palm trees grow on all the islands, so the design for this scarf is a palm leaf. The leaf pattern, cut from a stencil, can be used over and over again.

Materials and Tools

thin cotton fabric—½ yard of white,
   pale blue, or light yellow
sewing thread to match fabric
1 sheet of typewriter paper
1 sheet of stencil paper
1 sheet of cardboard—20 x 20 inches
acrylic paint—bright green
pencil
ruler
scissors
needle
pins
tools for cutting and coloring stencil

Directions

1. With the scissors, cut out a 17-inch square of fabric. Make a
¼-inch hem around the edges of the fabric by doubling ½ inch of
fabric over on itself. When hemmed, the fabric will measure 16 x 16
inches.
2. Enlarge the pattern by the grid method on the sheet of typewriter paper, using ruler and pencil.

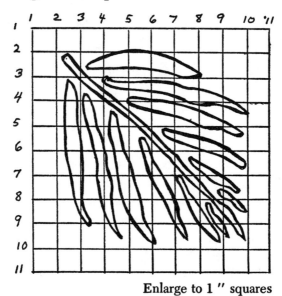

Enlarge to 1 ″ squares

3. Measure and cut a 9-inch square of stencil paper. Prepare the pattern and cut the stencil (see pages 117-118).

4. Once the stencil is cut, place it in position over the upper left corner of the cloth. Apply the paint through the cutout areas with the stencil brush.

5. Repeat the palm frond pattern three more times, as shown in the drawing. Let the paint dry between stencilings.

CHINESE PALM LEAF FAN

In China and the Far East, many fans are made from the lower part of a broad palm leaf, the edges bound with strips of reed, the leaf stem becoming the handle. The fans are often painted with designs—flowers, a pagoda, sprays of bamboo, a bird, or mountain scenes.

Palm leaf fans can now be bought in Oriental stores or in a dime store. In this project the fan is first covered with gold or brass colored metallic enamel, or gilt paint. The stenciled drum tower design is a copy of a thirteenth-century building, a type found all over China at that time. These towers were a combination of town gate and a place of warning by drum of attacks from outside.

Materials and Tools

1 sheet of typewriter paper
stencil paper—7 x 9 inches
sheet of cardboard—10½ x 13 inches
palm leaf fan—11 x 12¾ inches, 6-inch handle
2-ounce jar of metallic enamel—gold or brass
acrylic paint—black
acrylic polymer gloss medium
pencil
ruler
craft knife
flat nylon brush—¾ inch wide
tools for cutting and coloring stencil

Directions

1. Enlarge the drum tower pattern by the grid method on the sheet of typewriter paper. It will be 5½ inches wide and 6 inches long.

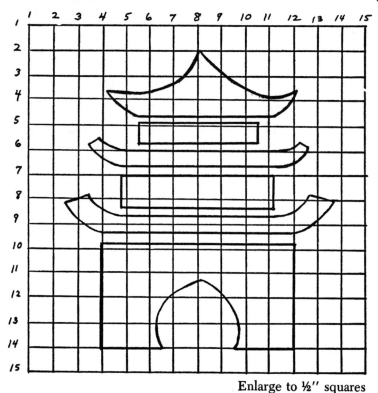

Enlarge to ½″ squares

2. Prepare the pattern and cut out the stencil with the craft knife (see pages 117-118).

3. Cover both sides of the palm leaf fan with metallic enamel, using the ¾-inch flat watercolor brush.

4. When the paint is dry, place the stencil over the center of the fan and hold it in place with small pieces of masking tape. The top of the design is 1 inch from the top edge of the fan. With the stencil brush, fill in the openings in the design with black acrylic paint. Remove stencil, and let the paint dry before moving the fan.

5. When the paint is dry, add a curved area of black paint at the base of the fan, using the ¾-inch flat brush. This area is 6 inches wide at the base, and 2¼ inches high in the center over the handle. Paint the handle with black paint. Let dry.

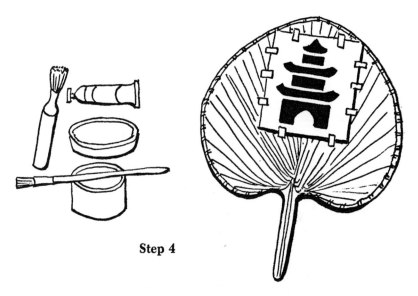

Step 4

6. With the ¾-inch flat brush, paint the stenciled side of the fan with acrylic polymer gloss medium. Let dry. Turn the fan over, and do the same on the other side. Also cover the handle with the acrylic polymer gloss medium. Let dry well before using the fan.

Variation: If you cannot find a palm leaf fan, substitute one made from a sheet of illustration board, using the drawing of the palm leaf fan as a guide. Use a piece of dowel split partway down its length for the handle. Insert the fan shape in the split and glue with contact cement.

SWEDISH BOOKENDS

In the eighteenth and early nineteenth centuries, painters traveled through the countryside of Sweden painting scenes on the walls in the houses of well-to-do people. These paintings were often scenes from the Bible or of royal persons. Decorative sprays of flowers and leaves were always added to each scene. The biblical scenes were all placed in a Swedish setting of the time. Joseph, going into Egypt, is riding in an open carriage, pulled by two elegantly stepping horses. Another scene shows the three Wise Men, dressed as officers of the Army or Navy, complete with cocked hats and swords.

The stenciled design on the bookends in this project is a flower and leaf design which was very popular at the time. The stencil forms the basic outline, and the rest of the design is added in a freehand style, just as the early Swedish painters did their wall decorations.

Materials and Tools

2 sheets of lightweight cardboard—12 x 16 inches
3 sheets of light blue construction paper—8 x 11 inches
3 sheets of typewriter paper
1 sheet of graphite paper
1 sheet of stencil paper
white household glue
acrylic paints—rust red, green,
    medium yellow, dark blue, and black
self-sticking (Mystic) tape—dark blue, ¾ inch wide
gravel or sand to fill bookends
acrylic polymer gloss medium, or polyurethane varnish
pencil
ruler
craft knife
small container
tools for cutting and coloring stencil
flat nylon brush—¾ inch wide
round nylon brush—#3
scissors
measuring spoons

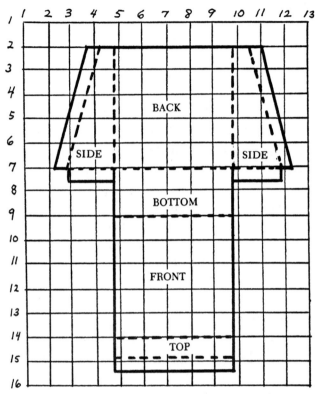

Enlarge to 1" squares

Directions

1. Enlarge pattern by the grid method on two sheets of typewriter paper glued together; transfer to the cardboard with graphite paper.

2. Cut the cardboard around the outside outline, using either scissors or craft knife. Lightly score the cardboard with the knife along the broken lines.

3. Fold the cardboard along the scored lines. Add glue to the flaps with the ¾-inch flat nylon brush. Put flaps in position and hold them in place on the inside with masking tape. Follow diagram numbers for the order of pasting each section into position. *Do not paste down the top section of each bookend.*

4. The cardboard is to be covered with the light blue construction paper. Measure and cut separate sections of construction paper to match each section of the cardboard bookends, except for the two front sections. The front sections will be stenciled, so you will need extra margins around these pieces—2 inches on all four sides.

5. Put 2 teaspoons of white glue in a small container or saucer, and add ¼ to ½ teaspoon of water, mixing well. Apply the glue with the ¾-inch brush to the back of a side section of construction paper. Put the section in its proper place on the bookend. Repeat with all the sections, except the two front ones which are to be stenciled.

6. Enlarge the stencil design on the typewriter paper by the grid method. Prepare the pattern and cut out the stencil (see pages 117-118).

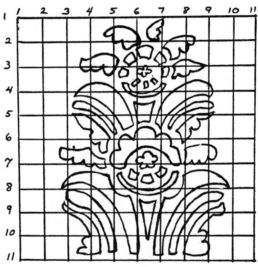

Enlarge to ½'' squares

7. Apply the basic colors of the design with the stencil to the two front sections of construction paper. The two pieces of light blue paper are larger than the front of the bookends, but the design is kept within the size of the front of the bookends. Stencil in each color as shown on the drawing. First brush in all the yellow areas; wash out the brush; fill in all the red areas, then the blue, and finally the green, washing out the brush between colors. When the colors are dry, outline the design parts and fill in the decorations with black. You can also pick your own colors.

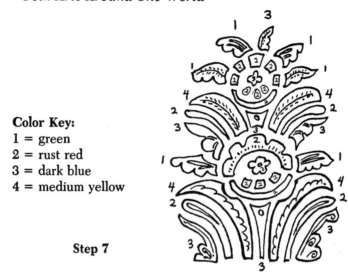

Color Key:
1 = green
2 = rust red
3 = dark blue
4 = medium yellow

Step 7

8. When the colored design is dry, cut the construction paper to the right size to fit the front of the bookends. Paste the two designs in place, one on each bookend as in Step 5.

9. Wait until the glue is dry before taping all the edges with the dark blue tape, following the drawing. Do all edges except the top.

10. Pour the gravel or sand into the bookends. Tape down the top.

11. Cover all parts of each bookend with the clear acrylic polymer gloss medium, or polyurethane varnish, using the ¾-inch flat nylon brush. Let dry before using the bookends.

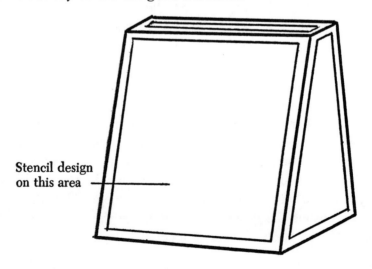

Stencil design on this area

Wood Folk Arts

❖ ❖ ❖

Techniques of Working with Wood

Using balsa wood

Balsa is a very soft, lightweight wood. It is easy to cut with a small craft saw, a jeweler's saw, or a sharp X-acto knife.

Balsa wood is sold in 36-inch long pieces; widths vary from 3 to 6 inches, with thicknesses of ⅛, ¼, and ½ inches. Balsa wood dowels also are 36 inches long.

All wood has a "grain." If you are using a sharp craft knife, it will be easy to cut with the grain. When cutting across the grain, you will have to make a series of shallow cuts, repeated along the same line so that the wood will not splinter or chip. Use an X-acto #19 blade in a #5 handle. Brace the knife against a ruler so the edge of the cut will be clean and even.

A clean cut can be made both with the grain and against the grain with a saw. The X-acto blades are #34, ¾ inch wide, and #35, 1 inch wide; both have a cutting edge 4½ inches long. They both fit into a #5 handle. The other type of craft saw is a jeweler's saw, which can also be used to cut metal, and to cut an "inside" shape without cutting through the outer edge of a piece of wood. This saw is described on page 80.

In all sawing, the cutting stroke is only one way; the return stroke of the saw does not cut into the wood. Some craft saw blades cut on the down stroke, others on the up stroke, so test the blade on scrap wood. A jeweler's saw blade is always held upright in its frame; the

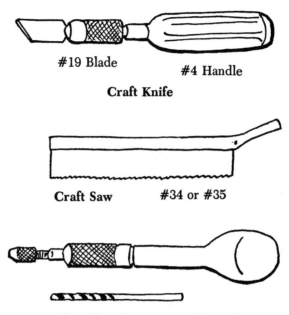

#19 Blade

#4 Handle

Craft Knife

Craft Saw   **#34 or #35**

Hand Drill and Wire Twist (or Bit)

cut is always made on the down stroke, as the teeth face downward.

All cut edges have to be smoothed with medium sandpaper and wood file, and the dust wiped off with a cloth or face tissue.

To make holes in the wood, use a hand drill with a bit the same size as the hole you want to drill. Bits are metal cylinders with a cutting edge; they come in many sizes and are set into the drill whenever needed.

All of the processes described in this section can be used on bass wood, which is a little harder than balsa wood, and on any other harder wood. You will find, though, that very hard woods are difficult to carve, and you will need stronger saw blades to cut through the tougher grain.

Using dowels

Dowels are lengths of wood which are shaped into circles, triangles, squares, or rectangles. Sizes vary from ⅛ inch to 2 or 3 inches across.

Balsa wood dowels in the smaller ⅛- to ¼-inch square or rectangular shapes can be soaked in water for two hours, then bent into a shallow curve. While the dowel is still wet, brace the curve with books, or thumbtacks stuck into a base and placed along the outside of the dowel. Let the wood dry thoroughly, and the curve will be permanent. Balsa wood is not as strong as the harder wood dowels.

Dowels of a harder wood are used when a project has to be supported from the dowels. For instance, a wall hanging may be stretched over a dowel, or a mobile may have objects hanging from a dowel.

Most hard wood dowels can be cut or carved with the same tools used for balsa wood. Use the craft saw to cut across the grain, which means cutting across the diameter of the dowel. The craft knife used for balsa wood is very good for carving or whittling. If you have to whittle out a section of a thicker dowel—1 to 3 inches or more—you can make a clean saw cut around the edge and then cut out the wood to that edge. You will also need a ⅜-inch wood gouge (#E X-acto), which also fits the #5 handle used in the balsa wood projects. This is used when going below the surface of the dowel.

Finishing wood

After you have finished carving or whittling and gouging the final object, go over the rough parts of the surface with a small wood file. Work over all areas until the surface is smooth. Follow the filing by rubbing all surfaces with medium sandpaper until the wood is satin smooth.

Finish the wood with a base coat of white shellac, polyurethane varnish, or clear acrylic polymer gloss medium, to seal the wood surface. This will keep the paint from soaking into the wood. Always put on two coats of this base varnish or shellac. Let the first coat dry, then sandpaper the surface lightly, dust off, and add the second coat. It is best to use a ¾-inch wide soft watercolor brush for the shellac, and a nylon brush for acrylic polymer gloss medium.

GERMAN NUTCRACKER PUPPET

A wooden nutcracker in the shape of a soldier was a popular household gadget in Germany in the early nineteenth century. In a story by E.T.A. Hoffmann, the Nutcracker is the hero of a little girl's dream on Christmas Eve. Years later, the story was made into the ballet "The Nutcracker." This project is also based on an old type of wooden puppet, known in Germany as a *Hampelmann* or Little Puppet. These have been favorite toys in Germany for many generations.

Color Key:
red = hat, jacket
yellow = epaulets, belt,
    buttons, braid trim on
    jacket and sleeves
black = boots, mustache,
    eyes, hair, mouth,
    lines of teeth
white = pants
pink (white + red) = face
    and hands

Materials and Tools
1 sheet of typewriter paper
1 sheet of graphite paper
balsa wood—8 x 3½ x ⅛-inch piece
fine sandpaper
white shellac
small jars of enamel paint—black, red,
   white, and yellow
6 tacks—½-inch long
black carpet thread—1 yard
pencil
ruler
scissors
craft saw or jeweler's saw
wood file
round watercolor brush—#3
flat watercolor brush—¾ inch wide
hammer
thin nail
hand drill and ¹⁄₁₆-inch bit (optional)

Directions
1. Use the grid method to enlarge the pattern to 8 inches long on the white typewriter paper. Transfer the enlarged pattern with graphite paper to the piece of balsa wood. Include pencil markings and tack holes.

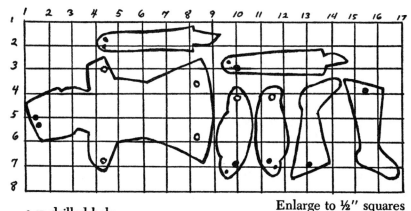

Enlarge to ½" squares

• = drilled hole
o = pencil mark

2. Cut out each piece with the saw. File any rough edges with a wood file. Smooth edges and flat surfaces with the sandpaper.

3. With either the thin nail and hammer or the drill and small bit, make holes at the pencil dots at the top of the head, each arm, upper leg, and lower leg. Smooth edges with sandpaper. The larger holes should be big enough so that the arms and legs will swing freely on the shanks of the tacks.

4. With the ¾-inch brush, paint all surfaces with white shellac. Keep the holes clear of liquid.

5. When shellac is dry, decorate the nutcracker with the enamel paints, using the #3 brush. Follow the color directions on the drawing.

6. Cut the black carpet thread into two pieces 8¼ inches long, and two pieces 6¾ inches long. One longer piece is tied to the top inside hole of one arm. The other longer piece is tied to the top inside hole of the other arm. One of the shorter pieces is tied to the top inside hole of the upper leg. The other shorter piece is tied to the top inside hole of the other upper leg.

7. Cut another piece of black thread, 4½ inches long. Pass it through the two holes at the top of the head, and tie the two ends together to form a loop to hang over your finger.

8. Make pencil dots on the back of the body at shoulder level and bottom edge, as well as the bottom edge of the upper legs, as shown in the pattern.

9. To attach the two halves of the legs to each other, and the legs and arms to the body, you will be using the six small tacks. Start with the legs. Place the upper leg flat on a working surface, painted side down. Put a tack through the hole in the lower leg. Place the point of the tack on the pencil dot at the lower end of the leg. Hammer the tack so that it holds in the wood, but does not come through to the painted surface. The lower leg should swing around freely on the tack. Repeat with the other leg. Then attach the two upper legs to the lower part of the body at the pencil marks in the same way. Finally attach the two arms to the two pencil marks at the top of the body at shoulder level.

10. Hold the nutcracker by the top loop. Smooth all the threads

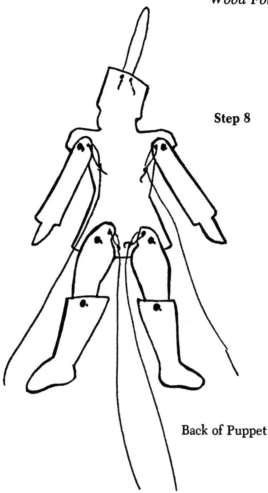

Step 8

Back of Puppet

downward and trim to the same length. Then tie small knots at the end of each thread. Now pull on each thread, or two threads or all four threads; the arms and legs will move up and down and the knees will bend.

MIDDLE EUROPEAN DOLL

All through Middle Europe, toys were made of wood. Wood was easy to find in the forests and easy to carve into simple shapes. Toys were made at home by fathers or grandfathers to amuse their families or to sell at the market. This type of simple doll was popular in Poland and Russia and other Middle European countries in the eighteenth and nineteenth centuries. Only the painted dress varied to match the local clothes.

Materials and Tools
1 sheet of typewriter paper
1 sheet of graphite paper
1 round wooden dowel—5¼ inches long,
    1¼ inches in diameter
1 round wooden dowel—2 inches long,
    ½ inch in diameter (Note: dowels are of basswood or other
    medium hard wood, not balsa wood.)
medium sandpaper
small jar of white shellac
acrylic paints—dark red, dark yellow,
    black, and white
file card—3 x 5 inches
2 tacks with ½-inch shanks
pencil
ruler
scissors
wood file
craft saw or jeweler's saw
2 round nylon brushes—#3 and #8
hammer
drawing compass

Directions
1. Draw a ½-inch circle in the center of one flat end of the 5¼-inch dowel. This end will be the top of the figure. At the other end, draw a line around the dowel, ³/₁₆ inch from the end. Draw a second line around the dowel, 1⅛ inches from the end.
2. With the wood file, starting at the top, begin filing away the wood from the ½-inch circle line at the top to the line 1⅛ inches from the bottom. You should have a long cone shape. When you

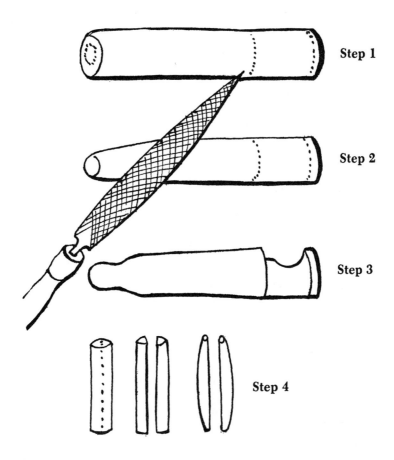

Step 1

Step 2

Step 3

Step 4

have finished this shaping, round off the ½-inch circle area at the top. Next, make a small, inward curve at the neck and shoulder area (see drawing).

3. The next area of filing will take a little longer. You will start at the line 1⅛ inch from the bottom. Cut into the dowel for ¼ inch and then file down the dowel for ⅝ inch, curving inward. Then slope outward to the $1/16$ inch line. This center area should look like legs close together.

4. Saw the 2-inch dowel in half *lengthwise* to make the two arms. Center a ¼-inch area at each end of the dowel. File away the wood in a gentle curve on the sides and top, ending at the ¼-inch mark, but not removing any wood at the center area. This center ½- to ⅝-inch section should remain ½ inch wide (see drawing).

5. Sandpaper and finish both the figure and the arms with shellac, using the #8 round nylon brush.

6. Enlarge the front and back pattern on the sheet of typewriter paper, using the grid method. Cut around the edges of the two patterns with the scissors.

Color Key:
dark red = dress, arms, lips, circles on scarf
dark yellow = scarf, decorations on front of dress, stripes on sleeves
black = stripes at bottom of dress, hair, eyes, eyebrows, nose, scarf lines, outlines of face and scarf
pink (white + red) = face

Enlarge to ½″ squares

7. When the shellac is dry, transfer the designs for the front and back (which includes the sides of the figure) to the wood with graphite paper.

8. Paint the figure and arms, following the colors shown on the pattern. Use the #8 round nylon brush for the overall color, and the #3 brush for the detailed pattern.

9. Let the figure and arms dry completely before adding the arms to each side. First, made a pencil dot on the outside of each arm, ⅝ inch down from the top. Make a pencil dot on each side of the figure. Using the hammer, drive a tack into each arm at the pencil mark. When the point of the tack appears on the opposite side of the arm, hold the arm against the side of the doll's body. The tack point should touch the pencil mark on the body. Drive the tack partway into the body. Insert a strip from the file card (folded four times over on itself) between the arm and the body. Drive the tack fully into the body. Remove the strip of file card. The thickness of the folded card has allowed just enough space between arm and body so the arm will swing easily into any position. Repeat with the other arm.

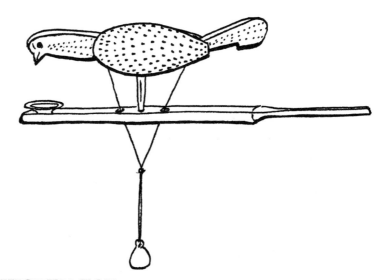

POLISH CHICKEN TOY

Craft designs have always reflected the life around the artist. Chickens were part of every farmyard in Poland and other Middle European countries, and so they became the models for the pecking-chicken toys found in this area. Sometimes there was just one chicken on the holding board; in other toys the craftsperson placed several chickens around the edge of a circular holding board, all attached to the one weight. These early animated toys kept children amused by the hour, and still do, as the toys are still made in these countries.

Materials and Tools
1 sheet of typewriter paper
1 sheet of graphite paper
round balsa wood or other soft wood dowel—
    2⅛ inches long, 1 inch in diameter
round balsa wood or other soft wood dowel—
    1¼ inches long, ¼ inch in diameter
balsa wood or other soft wood strip—
    8 x 2¼ x ¼ inches
acrylic paints—medium blue and light yellow
2 pieces of cotton cloth—4 x 4 inches
2 thin nails or brads—⅝ inch long
lead fishing weight—½ or 1 ounce
wood glue
plain concave button—1 inch in diameter
thin white string or carpet thread—14 inch length
2 felt-tipped pens—red and black (optional)
pencil
ruler
scissors
jeweler's saw
wood file
medium sandpaper
hand drill with ¼- and ⅜-inch bits
1 large pearl-headed pin or thin nail
2 small foil pans or paper cups for the paint

Directions
1. Enlarge the patterns for the holding board, the head, and the tail on the sheet of typewriter paper, using the grid method. Transfer patterns with graphite paper to the ¼-inch strip of balsa wood.

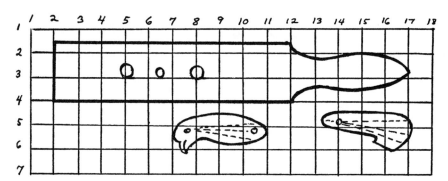

Enlarge to ½″ squares

2. Cut out the wood sections with a jeweler's saw. Smooth all surfaces with file and medium sandpaper. Thin out ½ inch of the narrow ends of the head and tail sections so they are only ³/₁₆ inch thick; this will allow them to fit easily into the slots in the body.

3. Drill three holes in the holding board: two holes are ⅜ inch wide; one hole is ¼ inch wide. See diagram for placement.

4. Form the piece of 1-inch diameter dowel into a long egg shape, using file and sandpaper. See drawing for shape.

5. With the jeweler's saw, cut out a slot at each end of the egg-shaped body; each slot is ⅝ inch long and a full ¼ inch wide. Smooth the cut surfaces. Drill a ⅜-inch diameter hole ⅜ inches deep into the bottom of the body. See drawing for placement. Set body to one side.

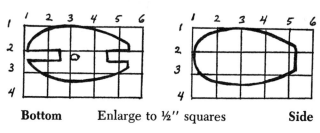

Bottom   Enlarge to ½″ squares   **Side**

6. Put the head and tail sections flat on the working surface. Lay the ruler over the wood, in position for the first line of the punched pattern. Make small holes in the wood with the point of the large pearl-headed pin, following the straight-line edge of the ruler. Repeat on the other side. Then repeat on both sides of the tail section. See drawing for design.

7. Make nicks in a circular pattern around the body, using the point of the scissors. See drawing on page 139.

8. Put an inch of medium blue acrylic paint in the mixing dish and add a little water. Mix well. Dip a small piece of cloth into the paint and then rub the sides of the body. The edges should fade so the top and bottom of the body are not covered with paint. If you have a black and a red felt-tipped pen, add an eye on each side with the black pen; the beak and eyebrow markings on each side are made with the red pen. If you do not have these pens, add the eyes, eyebrows, and beak marks with a toothpick dipped in the blue paint. Set aside to dry.

9. Mix about 2 inches of the yellow paint with water in a mixing dish. Dip the second piece of cloth in the paint, and rub the holding board with the paint until all surfaces are covered. Set aside to dry.

10. Make a hole at the thinned-out small ends of the tail and head sections, using a nail. The hole, 5/16 inch in from the end, should swing freely on the nail when tested. See diagram for placement. Attach a 7-inch length of white string or carpet thread to the hole at the end of the head section. Tie the other 7-inch length of thread to the hole at the end of the tail section.

11. Put the egg-shaped body flat on its side on the working surface. Gently hammer one nail through the narrow end of the body, 3/16 inch in from the end, until the point appears in the slot opening. Insert the tail into the slot, so the hole is opposite the nail, then continue to hammer gently. The nail will go through the hole and then into the opposite side of the slot. Hammer it in until the nail head is level with the wood body. Repeat with the head section, putting the nail into the body ¼ inch from the front end.

12. Smear wood glue into the center hole in the bottom of the body. Fit one end of the 1¼-inch long dowel into the hole. Let the glue dry. Cover the sides of the center hole in the holding board with glue. Hold the bird upright, and insert the other end of the dowel in the hole. Let the glue dry.

13. Put the head string through the front hole in the holding board, and the tail string through the other hole. Tie the two pieces of string together 1½ inches below the bottom of the holding board. Then tie the ends of the strings to the small fishing weight.

14. Finally, make a pencil dot on the spot on the holding board where the chicken's beak touches. Center the button on this pencil mark, and glue the button in place, concave side up. Let dry.

15. Grasping the holding board by the handle, move it sideways, back and forth, to start the weight swinging. The chicken will peck at the saucer as the tail moves up and down.

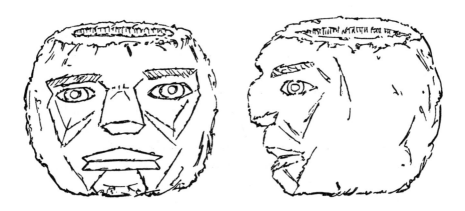

SOUTH PACIFIC TREE FERN POT

Tree ferns, which grow on the Pacific islands, have thick trunks that look like pressed-together twigs. The trunks are cut in sections, hollowed out, and used as pots to hold plants. The outside is often carved into a design. Because the material is dark brown and easy to carve, you can add a face like the Easter Island statues made of dark stone.

Materials and Tools
1 round tree fern pot—at least 5 inches in diameter and 4 inches high
2 white buttons—¼ to ⅜ inch in diameter
wood glue
craft knife or kitchen paring knife

Directions
1. Buy a tree fern pot at a garden center or plant store. It can be any size, from 5 inches in diameter and 4 inches high to 7 inches in diameter and 8 inches high. Whatever is the size of the pot, the carved design is the same. Just make a little bigger face on the larger pot.
2. Look at the drawing and copy the face by cutting into the surface. Start in the middle of the pot and carve out the nose. As you remove tree fern material, you will be forming the cheeks. Carve the cheeks back toward the sides of the pot. Carve out the eye area under the forehead. Make two oval cuts top and bottom for the eyes. Now remove material under the nose area for the lips and chin. Cut a deeper line for the mouth. The chin and jaw area is at the bottom of the pot.
3. With wood glue, add a white button to the center of each eye. In the Pacific islands this would be a small, white cowrie shell. If you have two of these shells, use them instead of buttons.
4. Add a plant in a plastic pot to the hole in the tree fern pot. The plant's plastic pot should just fit into the opening. Or put soil in the center opening and add a plant.

Sources for Supplies

✤ ✤ ✤

Here are listings of some mail-order craft and art supply companies. Send for their catalogs; then order any supplies which you cannot buy from your local stores. American Handicrafts (both catalog ordering and in their stores) and Dick Blick have a wide range of craft supplies, including paints, brushes, art paper, stencil paper, graphite paper, balsa wood boards and dowels, and all the other supplies and tools mentioned in this book.

Clay (Oven-baked)

American Handicrafts
3 Tandy Center
Fort Worth, TX 76102
(Repla-Cotta)

Sculpture House
38 East 30th St.
New York, NY 10016
(Della Robbia Clay)

Art Brown
2 West 46th St.
New York, NY 10036
(Miracle Clay)

Stewart Clay Company
133 Mulberry St.
New York, NY 10013
(Ceraclay)

Craft Saws and Knives

X-acto, Inc.
48-41 Van Dam St.
Long Island City, NY 11101

Fabric Printing

American Handicrafts
3 Tandy Center
Fort Worth, TX 76102
(Fabri-crylic)

Dick Blick
Box 1267
Galesburg, IL 61401
(Versatex Textile Paint,
Dorland's Textile Wax Resist)

Feathers and Beads

Grey Owl
Indian Craft Manufacturing Co.
150-02 Beaver Road
Jamaica, NY 11433

Metal Supplies and Tools

Allcraft
100 Frank Road
Hicksville, NY 11801

E. Jadow & Sons
53 West 23rd St.
New York, NY 10010

American Metalcraft, Inc.
4800 West Belmont Ave.
Chicago, IL 60641

TSI
487 Elliot Ave. West
Seattle, WA 98119

Griegers
900 S. Arroyo Pkwy.
Pasadena, CA 95470

Index

✤ ✤ ✤

ABOUT THE AUTHOR

VIRGINIE FOWLER's wide-ranging interests — in travel, collecting, and crafts — are brought together in this book. Her art school background has led her to explore all kinds of crafts, and her workroom is filled with jewelry-making tools, two enameling kilns, block-printing paraphernalia, and much more. On her travels through the Caribbean and Europe, she has visited craft centers, photographing and collecting local craft objects, and she has also studied and collected crafts from Africa and Asia.

A former children's book editor, Virginie Fowler is the author of several craft books for adults and children. With her husband George A. Elbert, she has written a number of books and articles on indoor plants and other subjects. The Elberts make their home in New York City.